THE 1950s

Music

1990s

1980s

1970s

1960s

1950s

1940s

1930s

1920s

1910s

1900s

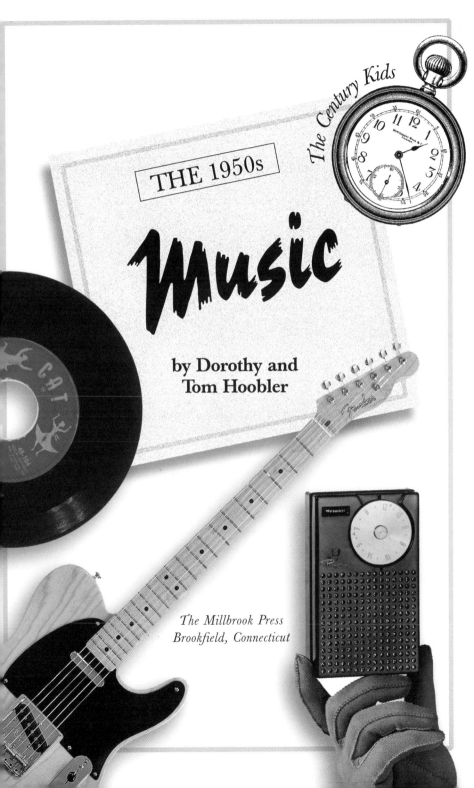

THE 1950s

The Century Kids

Music

by Dorothy and
Tom Hoobler

The Millbrook Press
Brookfield, Connecticut

Photographs courtesy of H. Armstrong Roberts: pp. 6, 19, 24, 26, 40, 84, 85, 91; AP/Wide World Photos: p. 7; FPG International: pp. 8, 35, 154 (Jeanne); Archives Photos: p. 9 (NBC Television); Gryphon Records: p. 12; Underwood Photo Archives, Inc.: pp. 13, 15, 88; Private collection: p. 18; © Corbis/Bettmann: pp. 27, 46, 89, 90, 146; © Fender Musical Instruments Corp.: p. 29; Brown Brothers: pp. 30, 42 (both), 110 (both); Quarter Master Museum: p. 31; Anne Canevari Green: p. 33; Ginger Giles: p. 34; © UPI/Corbis-Bettmann: pp. 47, 71, 139, 145; Michael Ochs Archive.com: pp. 50 (© Ray Flerlage), 79, 83, 128; Chicago Historical Society: p. 52 (ICHi-30055); March of Dimes: p. 56; Morse Telegraph Club, Inc.: p. 64; Lake County (IL) Museum, Curt Teich Postcard Archives: p. 77; McDonald's Corporation: p. 82; Culver Pictures, Inc.: p. 99; National Archives: p. 138

For Fred and Eleanor Law

Hoobler, Dorothy.
The 1950s: music/by Dorothy and Tom Hoobler.
p. cm.—(The century kids)
Summary: In the 1950s Matthew befriends a Negro boy
who introduces him to the new music, and
together they start a rock-and-roll band.
ISBN 0-7613-1605-1 (lib.bdg.)
[1. Bands (Music)—Fiction. 2. Rock music—Fiction.
3. Afro-Americans—Fiction.] I. Hoobler, Thomas. II. Title.
PZ7.H76227 Aac 2001
[Fic]—dc21 00-045088

Published by The Millbrook Press, Inc.
2 Old New Milford Road
Brookfield, Connecticut 06804
www.millbrookpress.com

Two Birthdays

JANUARY 1, 1950

ROCCO'S FAMOUS ITALIAN RESTAURANT WAS Matthew's favorite place to eat. His dad used to take the whole family there often, especially on Wednesday nights. That was when *Charley's Chat* was broadcast live on the radio from the restaurant. Dad was the show's producer.

But they hadn't gone to Rocco's for nearly a year. *Charley's Chat* had been taken off the air because Charley had defended his mother, Peggy Aldrich. Matthew's dad got in trouble too—not just because he was the producer of *Charley's Chat*, but because Peggy Aldrich was his cousin.

As far as Matthew could tell, it all happened because Peggy was a Communist sympathizer. At least that was what the newspapers called her.

Peggy

They hadn't seen Peggy since, but she would be here today. All their relatives would be. It was going to be a dual birthday celebration. Both Rocco Vivanti and Nell Aldrich, Peggy's sister, were fifty years old today.

Dad had warned Matthew not to say anything about the Communist sympathizer trouble. He said he wouldn't, but he figured somebody else would. Practically everybody was talking about the congressional hearings. Matthew had watched them on television. Most of the time they were pretty boring, but of course when somebody you knew was being investigated, you had to watch. Anyway, there were only three channels, and all three were carrying the hearings.

The House Un-American Activities Committee was looking for Communists. Especially if they were in the entertainment industry. Peggy wrote screenplays and had even directed a few movies, even though she was working for a newspaper now. Earlier in the hearings, somebody had said she was a Communist, so the committee called on her to tes-

A House Un-American Activities Committee hearing

tify. That was the way the hearings went: You had to name all the people you knew who you thought were Communists, even if you weren't one yourself.

Peggy denied that she was a Communist. But she refused to answer when the committee asked her if she knew any Communists. She said she wasn't brought up to gossip in public about her friends. That made the committee pretty mad, and she was cited for contempt, whatever that meant.

Peggy went to jail for a few days, but when she got out she said that she still had contempt for the committee. So besides going to jail she lost her job with the newspaper and wasn't allowed to write for the movies, either.

Charley

That was when Charley, her son, devoted one of his radio shows to attacking the committee. He didn't tell anybody what he was going to do. He just spoke by himself for an hour, expressing his contempt for the committee too and saying that its members were the people who were really un-American.

Naturally he lost his job. The network and the sponsor got a lot of letters from people who said they didn't want any Communist sympathizers on the radio.

Matthew's dad was almost fired too. The network moved him over to producing television shows, because nobody cared as much about them. He was assigned to develop a show for kids, which was what he was doing now.

Carol, Matthew's little sister, told him he should make it like *The Howdy Doody Show*. She watched it every day after school. Howdy Doody was a puppet with a human friend called Buffalo Bob Smith. Each afternoon at 5:30, Buffalo Bob started the show by asking, "Say, kids! What time is it?" And the studio audience—which was all kids, sitting in what they called the Peanut Gallery—yelled out, "It's Howdy Doody time!" So did Carol and probably a couple million kids in

It's Howdy Doody Time!

front of their TV sets everywhere. Matthew didn't like to admit it, but he watched the show too.

Anyway, Dad just said he was working on an idea for a show. That meant he hadn't come up with one yet. "I'm thinking of bringing Nell to television," he said.

Matthew didn't say anything but he felt that wasn't a good idea. Nell had been a big movie star once, but she was sort of over the hill now. Her cousin Harry was a bigger star, even though he was older than she was. He played action roles like sea captains, cowboys, and war heroes. Matthew liked Harry's movies way more than any of Nell's.

The kids at Matthew's school thought it was neat that he was related to real movie stars. But it wasn't all that great. Harry Aldrich was the sort of person who was always looking for a mirror so he could check how he looked. Outside the movies, he wasn't very interesting. Dad said if nobody wrote lines for him, he didn't have anything to say. And when you got up close to him, you saw he was older than he looked in the movies. Mom said once that she thought he wore a girdle to keep his tummy in.

Nell was a little different. She was nice to everybody. Matthew and Carol had stayed at her house in California during the summer. She enjoyed having kids around, probably because she had never married. Matthew could see how people used to think she was beautiful. If Matthew were really old, maybe as old as Dad, he might have thought she still was.

By the time they arrived at Rocco's, the party was going strong. The restaurant was hardly big enough to hold everybody. Rocco had a million friends, and of course a lot of show business people came because they wanted to see Nell.

Even before they got their coats off, Charley came running up. Matthew had never liked his radio show that much. Charley liked to use big words and act like he was smart. Well, probably he was smart. Everybody said so. And of course he was brave because he defended his mother even though it caused him to lose his job. He was just so roly-poly he didn't look very brave.

"Freddy," Charley said, shaking hands with Dad, "I've got to talk with you. I've come up with a great idea for a show."

Dad looked around. "The network isn't ready to let you back, Charley."

"They won't even know I'm involved," Charley told him. "I've got a way to get around that."

"Well . . . a little later," said Dad. "We've got to say hello to Nell and Rocco."

They found Rocco first, sitting at a table with a glass of red wine and surrounded by half a dozen friends. Matthew recognized the mayor of Chicago among them.

Carol ran to give Rocco the present they'd brought. It was a record album of Verdi's *Aida*, one of Rocco's favorite operas. Mom called to Carol not to drop the album; any of the eight records inside it could break easily.

Rocco unwrapped it and showed it for everybody at the table to see. "You didn't have to bring

me anything," he said. "Look at all I got already." He waved his hand and they understood what he meant—his restaurant, his friends, his family. . . .

"Hey," Rocco said to Dad, "one thing is missing. On Wednesday nights, you know, it seems empty in here. People used to come for Charley's show. When you gonna come up with another one?"

"Rocco," said Dad, "I'm doing my best."

"Work a little harder," Rocco said. "That's what I tell myself whenever things get hard.

Remember that night we listened to the *Titanic*? I never thought I'd get through it. I just told myself I had to."

"I remember, Rocco," Dad said. "But things were simpler then. This is harder."

"Hey, the Depression was hard too," Rocco told him. "And World War II." He put his hand on Matthew's arm. "You're a lucky kid," he told him, "You didn't have to go to war. Your father never had to worry about you."

Rocco

Rocco looked back at Dad. "Freddy," he said. "All this Communist stuff . . . it's going to blow over. Don't pay any attention to it."

The mayor of Chicago leaned over and said something in Rocco's ear. "Yeah?" said Rocco. "You think so? I gotta be careful what I'm saying in my own restaurant now?" He shook his head. "Maybe you're right, Freddy. I should be the one to worry. Because I thought this was America."

Everybody laughed nervously. Dad shook hands with Rocco and moved away from the table. "Teresita set out some snacks for anybody who's hungry," Rocco called after them. "But save room for when we all sit down to dinner."

"Can I go get some of the food?" Matthew asked his mother. He could hardly wait.

"Not yet," she told him. "Wait till we say hello to Nell."

As they made their way through the crowd, they met other friends of Dad's. They stopped to chat, making Matthew more impatient to get into the other room and start on what Rocco called snacks. Matthew hoped there would be plenty of the stuffed clams. This was the only place where he ever ate clams; Mom never made them at home. And in the one other restaurant where Matthew had seen clams on the menu, they didn't taste anything like Rocco's. Mom said that was because Rocco's were stuffed with a lot more than clams.

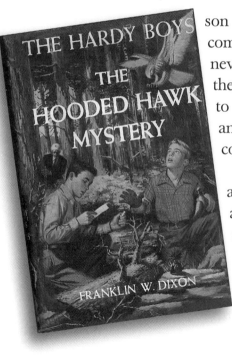

The food was the only reason that Matthew wanted to come to the party, really. There never seemed to be anybody there his own age. He wanted to bring a Hardy Boys book and read it while he ate, but of course Mom wouldn't let him.

It wouldn't have made any difference, since all the adults mostly ignored him and said how pretty Carol was. Matthew was used to that—everybody thought so. Mom was talking about sending Carol for acting or tap dance lessons.

Finally they reached Nell's table. She was sitting with four little boys, all of whom looked three or four years old. Nell was dealing cards to each one. She looked up when Matthew's family arrived. "Freddy! Silvia!" she said to Dad and Mom. "I'm so glad you could come. And I'm delighted to see you brought the children." Matthew shifted back and forth from one foot to the other as Nell looked him over. "We're playing go fish," she said. "Anyone want to join us?"

Nell

Fortunately, he didn't have to answer because Carol piped up, "We brought you a present."

"Oh, you did that just to remind me I was fifty," Nell said, making believe she was cross. "I don't need anything more."

Matthew remembered that was the same thing Rocco had said. Was it true? Did you get so old that there wasn't anything more that you wanted? He thought about Dad—he was a year older than Rocco and Nell, but Matthew knew Dad still wanted to buy a boat and sail it on Lake Michigan in the summertime.

Still, Nell took the present and showed the gaily wrapped box to the boys around the table. They clapped. "Can we have cake now?" one of them asked.

"We have to wait a little while longer," Nell said. She looked up. Her bright blue eyes reminded Matthew of somebody. Then he realized: His sister Carol had the same kind of eyes, only younger.

Nell saw it too. "What's your name, dear?" she asked.

"Carol."

"A pretty name . . . Carol Woods." She said it aloud a couple times, trying out the way it sounded. "Do you have a middle name?"

"Anne."

"Anne . . . Carol Anne. Almost there." Nell thought for a second. "What do you think of Carol Lee Woods?"

Mother interrupted. "Anne was my grandmother's name."

Nell's eyebrows went up. "Oh! Well then, it had better stay Carol Anne, hadn't it?"

Matthew laughed. There was something funny in the way Nell had said it. But he shut up quickly when Mom gave him a look.

"Aren't you going to open the present?" asked Carol. She was only eight years old, so Mom wasn't always warning *her* to be polite.

But Matthew was just as curious to know whether Nell would like the present. Both he and Carol knew that Dad had bought something they couldn't really afford. The change in jobs meant they had to cut back, Mom was always telling them. That meant Dad wasn't getting paid as much.

He had bought Nell a silver bracelet with blue stones from someplace in the Andes Mountains. Nell had made a movie there a couple of years ago. She had apparently liked the scenery. Her cousin Polly had taken her way up in the mountains and showed Nell an ancient Inca city. It made a big impression on her.

Dad had a reason for buying the bracelet. He was good at getting people to do what he wanted. And he wanted something from Nell. Matthew had overheard Mom telling him, "Oh, Freddy, Nell would never do *that*!"

But Dad said, "You never know with Nell. She's always made up her own mind. And if she likes the show, she'll do it."

So that was why they all wanted Nell to open the present. But Nell said, "It looks so pretty, I think I'll leave it wrapped for now. That way I can enjoy it more. Why don't you sit down here by me, Carol Anne? Two of these boys are cousins of yours. Can you guess which ones?"

Matthew looked around the table along with Carol. They both laughed, because one, at least, was easy to spot. "Him," Carol said, pointing to a boy who looked exactly like a miniature Charley Norman.

Chuck

"Yes," said Nell. "That's Charles Norman III, only I've dubbed him Chuck. That might give him a better start when he gets to school."

"And him," said Carol, pointing to another of the boys. "Only I'm not as sure, except I think the others must be Rocco's children."

"Well, the one you pointed out is Harry's son Dick, named for his grandfather who went down on the *Titanic*. Harry and his new wife are off traveling, so I brought Dick to my birthday party." She nudged Dick, who looked as if he were falling asleep.

"Having a good time, Dick?" she asked. His dark hair fell down in his eyes, and she brushed it back. "I think Dick may be coming down with something. Anyway, the last two are not Rocco's children. They're his grandchildren. This is Arturo, or Art, the younger, and here's Michelangelo, definitely Mike, the elder by a year. Both of them are Tony's sons. His wife likes fancy names."

She shuffled the cards and began to deal. "That was the one thing I didn't have—children. So you see, now that I'm able to, I take other people's children. I have all the fun that way."

"Why didn't you have children?" Carol asked. From the look on Dad's face, Matthew guessed it wasn't the right question to ask.

Nell didn't seem offended. She smiled and said, "Well, dear, here's a secret. The man I should have married got away from me. And nobody else ever seemed good enough."

"Who was he?"

"Oh," Nell said with a little smile, "*I'll* never tell."

Dick

"But you're a star," Carol said. "You could have married . . . , " she spread her arms, ". . . just about anybody you wanted."

Nell looked at Carol and said, "I hope you don't find out what I have, dear. Being rich and famous is not what it's cracked up to be."

So, thought Matthew with relief. Even if you were old like Nell, there were still some things you still wanted. You just wouldn't tell anybody.

A Surprise Announcement

JANUARY 1, 1950

MATTHEW MANAGED TO GET OUT OF PLAYING GO fish. He wandered into the room where platters of food had been set out. Just the smell of cheese and salami was enough to make Matthew hungry, and he'd skipped lunch anyway because he knew they were going to Rocco's.

Even so, the plate of food he assembled looked puny compared to the one at the table where he sat down. *That* gigantic feast—chunks of fresh mozzarella as large as baseballs and six-inch-high stacks of sliced salami and mortadella—sat in front of cousin Charley.

"You're Matthew, if I'm not mistaken," Charley said in between bites.

Matthew nodded. He was rolling thin slices of sweet salami around dabs of ricotta cheese.

"What kind of program is your father planning at CBN television?" Charley asked. "Has he envisioned anything serious? Aimed at exploiting the cultural possibilities of a new medium?"

Matthew hadn't the slightest idea. "He wants to talk to Nell about doing a show with her," he replied.

Charley's eyebrows went up. "Nell? She would never agree. No television producer could afford to pay her a fraction of what she gets for a movie."

Matthew bit into one of the salami and ricotta rollups. When he was about six, Rocco's daughter Gabriella had showed him how to make these. Every time he came to Rocco's, this was what he ate for the antipasto. "Yeah," he mumbled, "but Dad says Nell's . . ." He decided he'd better not tell Charley what Dad had said.

Charley guessed anyway. "That she's past her prime? That may be, but she still has important roles now and then. Nell is old Hollywood royalty, and it would be a step down for her to appear on television. Most of the people in Hollywood think television is just a fad—sort of like adding a small picture to a radio. Not a very clear picture, at that."

"So if that's true," said Matthew, "how come *you* want to be on television."

Charley sliced a piece of his mozzarella base-ball and put it between two tomatoes. They were the tomatoes that Rocco grew himself, that you couldn't buy anyplace else. "There are two reasons, actually," Charley said. "First is that I am perceptive enough to recognize the possibilities inherent in this new form of information and entertainment. The people who run the movie business are living in the past. They're dinosaurs, with big bodies and tiny brains. Ten years from now, all the movie theaters will be closed." He put the tomato/mozzarella sandwich on a slice of toasted garlic bread and took a large bite out of it.

"And what's the second reason?" asked Matthew.

"The second reason," said a soft voice behind him, "is that Charley needs a job and television is his best chance."

The owner of the voice, a tall, slender Negro woman, sat down at the table.

"Oh, hello, Lorraine," said Charley. "Were you listening in on our private conversation?" he asked with a pout.

"That's right, Charley," she replied. "Of course it helped that you were speaking loudly enough that half the people in the room could hear you."

Lorraine

"I inadvertently assume my broadcasting voice when I'm here at Rocco's," said Charley. "Old habits die hard."

Lorraine offered her hand to Matthew. Surprised, he took it and was even more surprised at how strong her grip was. "I'm Lorraine Dixon Wilkins," she said. "I made Charley famous the first time."

Charley laughed and said, "You were lucky. Anyway, I became America's best-loved chat moderator on my own."

"Really?" said Lorraine. She glanced sideways at Matthew, giving him a wink. "Aren't you Freddy Woods's son?"

"That's right," said Matthew.

"Ask your father who put Charley on the radio."

Matthew didn't have to. He knew Dad had done that.

"It doesn't matter now," Charley said, with a tone of discouragement. "Since I've lost my job."

"Well, Charley," said Lorraine, "you have only your own stubbornness and courage to thank for that."

"Maybe if I had better legal counsel," Charley shot back, "I wouldn't have been fired."

Lorraine looked at Matthew. "I was Charley's lawyer," she said. "But he forgets that he couldn't find another lawyer willing to defend Communist sympathizers."

"You'll defend anyone," Charley said. Matthew suddenly realized that even though Charley and Lorraine seemed to be arguing, they really liked each other a lot.

"I defend anyone who *needs* defending," said Lorraine. "But I'm proud of you, Charley. When the time came to stand up and be counted, you did it. A lot of people today are running from anyone who points a finger and yells, 'Communist!'"

Charley shrugged. "It was my mother they were accusing."

"Where is Peggy, anyway?" asked Lorraine.

"She's hiding."

"Hiding? She didn't come to her own sister's birthday party?"

"She's here, but she's staying out of sight. She's worried that somebody will take her picture with Nell and that will hurt Nell's career."

"That wasn't Nell's idea, I'm sure."

"No, but Mother thinks Nell still can't take care of herself."

Just then a little girl ran up to the table and put her arms around Lorraine's knees. "Mommy," she said. "Michelle and Ronnie are going to play music and they won't let me."

"Well, your cousins have had lessons, Sojie," said Lorraine. "Charley, did you ever meet my daughter Sojie?"

"Sojie?" Charley repeated as if he wasn't sure he heard it right.

Sojie

"Her real name is Sojourner Truth Wilkins. We got a little carried away when she was born, so now we call her Sojie for short."

Charley smiled. "If she's like you she's going to insist on getting what she wants."

"I hope so," said Lorraine. She turned in her chair and looked toward the bandstand at the front of the room. A boy and a girl close to Matthew's age were playing with some of the instruments that the band had left. The boy was tapping on the drum set and the girl was tooling on a saxophone.

"Matthew," said Lorraine, "would you mind going up there and telling those two that their Aunt Lorraine would like to see them?"

Matthew did as she asked. He was a little hesitant. He didn't know any colored kids. There weren't any in his school, but he heard they were tough. Still, they looked a year or two younger than he was. He figured he could handle them, particularly since Lorraine was nearby.

When he stepped onto the bandstand, the girl looked at him without putting down the saxophone. She made it bleat like a sheep; Matthew had the feeling she was making fun of him. Without going any closer, he pointed to Lorraine's table. "Your aunt says she wants to talk to you," he said.

The girl made some more sounds on the saxophone. Matthew recognized the echo of his own voice in the notes.

Then there came a RAT-A-TAT SPANGGGG! on the drums, with a cymbal crash at the end. He looked over to see the boy grinning at him, a drumstick in each hand.

"Your aunt," he said loudly and distinctly, "wants . . . to . . . see . . . you."

"Can't she see us from where she's sittin'?" asked the boy. His sister took the saxophone out of her mouth just long enough to give a high-pitched one-syllable laugh: "Ha!"

Matthew shrugged. He'd delivered the message. He looked around. He had to admit it was kind of neat being up here with all the instruments lying around. If only he had the nerve to pick up one of them—but of course he'd get caught by somebody and Dad would yell at him.

A sleek-looking red guitar was leaning against a chair. It wasn't like any guitar Matthew had ever seen before. A rubber cord led from the side of it to a loudspeaker set on the floor.

"Hey," the boy at the drums called to him. "You play the guitar?"

Matthew looked at him and shook his head no.

"You never know till you try," the boy urged him. "Go 'head, pick it up."

Matthew smiled to show he'd like to.

"G'wan," the boy repeated. "It's all right. It belongs to my Daddy."

"Really?" Matthew asked.

"Well, kind of. It's his band playin' here today. Rocco likes jazz."

Hesitantly, Matthew reached down and picked up the guitar. It was heavier than he'd expected. He slipped the strap over his head and let the guitar hang from his neck. He strummed his fingers over the steel strings.

Nothing happened.

"You gotta turn it on," the boy told him. "It's electric."

Sure, Matthew thought. That was why there was a cord. He'd read about electric guitars. They were brand-new. He'd never heard anybody play one.

Matthew found the switch. "Turn that knob too," the boy at the drums called to him. "Turn it way up as far as it goes."

Matthew nodded. He understood it now. He held the guitar neck tightly and used his other hand to strum the strings. . . .

WAAAANNNNNGGG!! A deafening crash came from the loudspeaker sitting on the floor directly behind Matthew.

Everybody in the room looked up startled. It took Matthew a second to realize they were looking straight at him.

He heard the boy at the drums laughing—not a one-syllable laugh like the girl's. No, he sounded as if someone would have to dunk him in a tank of ice water to get him to stop.

Lorraine was out of her chair and headed straight for the stage, looking as though she was more than ready for a little talk.

But despite everything, Matthew had only one thought: I've *got* to get one of these electric guitars.

Much later in the evening, Matthew sat at the back of the ballroom with Ronnie and Michelle, the two kids from the bandstand. The real band had returned—and in fact, their father was the band-leader. He played the piano pretty good too. Out on the floor, couples were dancing. Michelle had tried to persuade her brother, and then even Matthew, to dance the jitterbug. She told Matthew she'd show him how, but like her brother he turned

her down. In fact, both boys were so stuffed with food they didn't even feel like moving.

Matthew was surprised. He couldn't have imagined that he would make friends with a colored boy, but he and Ronnie were interested in the same things. Of course, Matthew liked the Cubs and Ronnie rooted for the White Sox. But both of them hated the New York Yankees more than anything.

They collected uniform patches from World War II army units too. Both of them had big collections. They decided maybe they'd get together and trade duplicates.

Just as Matthew thought it was neat that Ronnie's father was a bandleader, Ronnie said it was cool that Matthew's father worked in television. Matthew had never heard anybody use the word *cool* in just that way before. He was also surprised to learn that Ronnie and Michelle's family, the Greens, didn't even have a TV yet. They went downstairs in the apartment building to watch a neighbor's set.

One thing Matthew found almost too much to believe. In fact, the boys nearly got into a fight about it. Ronnie said his Uncle Marcus drew the Masked Crusader comic books. Matthew avoided saying it at first, but he didn't believe a colored person could draw a comic strip with a white hero.

But when he *did* say it, Ronnie replied, "The Masked Crusader isn't white. He's colored."

"Come on," said Matthew. "I mean, of course he's white."

"How do you know?"

"Well . . . it's obvious. Just look at him."

"You can't see his face. It's covered with a mask."

Matthew thought for a second. "Well, you can see his *hands*."

"No, you can't. He always wears gloves."

Maybe that was right. Matthew couldn't remember if the Masked Crusader wore gloves or not. "Well, I know he's white," he insisted.

They settled it by finding Charley and Lorraine. "Yes," Charley agreed, "Marcus is a very talented artist and always has been. He draws comic books, but he also paints very interesting canvases that have not yet attracted the attention of the art world."

"And he's Ronnie's uncle?" asked Matthew.

"Yes, he's the brother of Ronnie and Michelle's mother, Nancy."

"And that means . . ." Matthew started to say, but then got embarrassed because Lorraine was sitting there.

She understood and laughed. His ears burned. "Matthew," said Lorraine, "you have just been let in on one of the world's biggest secrets. The

THE MASKED CRUSADER

Masked Crusader is in fact a Negro. But you can't tell anyone, promise?"

He promised. Nobody he knew would believe him anyway. But he was curious: "Why not?"

"Because then he'll get kicked out of comic books and have to go work in the post office." Lorraine and Charley found this funny, but Matthew didn't get it.

Anyway, the dancing finally stopped and the musicians played a fanfare. The mayor of Chicago went up on the bandstand and gave a little speech about his friend Rocco Vivanti, and his wonderful

Gabriella

family, and how much the Italians had given to the great city of Chicago, which was also honored today by having one of Hollywood's greatest stars . . . and so on.

Matthew sort of stopped listening until finally Rocco and Nell stepped forward. The kitchen doors opened at the same time and Rocco's daughter Gabriella came out carrying a three-tier cake with fifty candles blazing. As she marched toward the bandstand, everybody in the room stood and sang Happy Birthday.

Together, Rocco and Nell leaned over and blew out the candles. All but one, which stubbornly kept bursting into flame even after they thought it was out. Rocco licked two fingers and snuffed out the candle with them. The guests applauded and then began to call for a speech.

Rocco looked at Nell, but she nudged him forward. Finally he cleared his throat and said loudly,

"Hey, you got the biggest movie star in the world here—and you want *me* to speak? All I want to say is, I look around this room and see my friends, my sons and daughters, my wife . . . hey! where's Teresita?"

"She ran off with another guy," yelled somebody in the crowd. That brought a roar of laughter.

"Naw," Rocco said. Gabriella tugged at his arm and pointed.

Teresita

Teresita stood at the kitchen door, wearing an apron with white-flour handprints on it. "There she is," Rocco said. "Come on up, Teresita." But she just shook her head.

Matthew remembered hearing Dad ask Mom, "Wonder if Teresita's going to bake a cake that says 'Happy Birthday, Rocco' and forget to put Nell's name on it." Mom shushed him when she realized Matthew was in the next room and could hear them.

"My best friend in the world," Rocco was saying now, looking at Nell. "If it wasn't for her and her sister, I probably would still be working in a mill in Massachusetts." He looked out at the room. "Where's Peggy?" he asked, and the room fell silent.

Nell stepped to the edge of the bandstand. "Yes, Peggy, come up here. We want you with us."

35

Then people to Matthew's left started to turn and look. A thin woman with dark hair streaked with gray was walking toward the bandstand. Matthew stood on a chair so he could see her better. She looked different from the way she had on television and in the newspapers. Not so scary.

Someone started to applaud. Matthew saw it was Charley and Lorraine. Others began to join in. So did he, not really knowing why. Communist sympathizers should be shipped off to Russia, he knew. The *Chicago Tribune* said so. But if Rocco liked Peggy so much, maybe she wasn't really a Communist sympathizer.

Finally Peggy stood on the bandstand and Nell put her arms around her. Some flashbulbs popped at the front of the room. A few people booed but the rest of the crowd drowned them out with applause. Nell raised her hands for quiet.

"My sister has always been part of everything I've done," she said. "All my successes . . . and if there were any failures, it wasn't her fault." That drew some laughs. "And I want to let you all in on a secret."

The crowd hushed. "Most of you know I haven't made many movies lately. Or at least not many that people wanted to *see*." More laughter, not so loud.

"I thought it was time for me to retire . . ." Nell went on.

Shouts of "No! No!" came from the crowd.

Nell smiled. "Well, tonight I agreed to do something new. My cousin Freddy Woods—who most of you know—has persuaded me to star in a television show."

Surprised gasps echoed around the room. Nell must have liked the bracelet, Matthew thought.

"Now, if my cousin Harry were here, he'd tell me television's just a fad," Nell went on. "But then I remembered almost forty years ago when Harry's father and my parents and grandparents were all actors in the theater. They said movies were just a fad too. And then I met D. W. Griffith, and you know what happened."

Laughter and applause, for what happened was that Nell became one of the biggest stars of the silent movies.

"Well, I've decided to try my hand at something new. You see this cake? It represents the first fifty years of my life. And the *next* fifty . . ." she paused for the laughter, ". . . will be the icing on the cake."

THREE

Going Nowhere

OCTOBER 1951

MATTHEW LIKED TO DO HIS HOMEWORK IN FRONT of the television set. At first Mom didn't want him to sit so close to it because she'd heard that radioactive beams came out of the picture tube.

But Dad told her that the network had done studies proving that watching television raised children's IQ's. And if there *was* any radioactivity inside the tube, it couldn't harm you.

Anyway, Dad wanted Matthew to keep the set on, at least between 4:30 and 5:00 in the afternoon. That was when *The Aunt Nell and Huckleberry Show* was on. And of course, the more people who watched it, the more sponsors it would get.

To Matthew the show was babyish, but almost everybody on it was a relative of his. Besides, it helped him concentrate on his homework.

Auntie Nell was, of course, Nell Aldrich. The format of the show was to surround her with kids and see what happened. Some days she would play games with them; other times she read a story. When she read a story the screen might show cartoon characters acting out the scenes from the book.

Huckleberry

Then there was Huckleberry. He was a clown who came onto the show to mess things up. He carried an old pocket watch and was always looking at it, trying to rush Nell through the story. Sometimes he would interrupt by asking dumb questions. *Real* dumb questions that were so idiotic they made the kids laugh.

When Huckleberry caused too much trouble, Auntie Nell would have to punish him by making him sit in a corner or wear a dunce cap. Of course that didn't stop him for long. He would sneak away and when the kids saw him, they would yell and point him out to Aunt Nell.

Huckleberry was actually Charley Norman. Nobody knew that except Matthew's dad, Nell, and a few other people. It had to be a secret because people who defended Communist sympathizers—even their mothers—weren't allowed on TV.

Matthew's dad said Nell had only agreed to do the show if Charley was hired too. Charley had planned something quite different. He had wanted to do a Mystery Critic show in which he was the mystery critic. Wearing a disguise, he would talk about new books, plays, and movies.

Wearing clown makeup was only another kind of disguise. But Charley hadn't been so keen on the idea at first. Eventually he came around, because as Dad said, "A job is a job."

Nell convinced Charley to give it a try. She told him, "You're really an Aldrich, like me and even like Harry. Acting is in your blood."

"This isn't acting," Charley complained.

"Oh, but it *is*," she replied. "One of the nineteenth-century Aldriches, grandfather's older brother Francis, specialized in comedy roles. He was famous for playing Sir John Falstaff in Shakespeare's historical plays. By the way, that role would suit you too."

Charley was flattered by that, and agreed to put on the Huckleberry suit. Everybody agreed that he really was a natural for the role. Matthew's sister Carol told him that the kids on the show really liked it when Huckleberry said something dumb.

Carol was part of the show too. She was one of Aunt Nell's Kids. At first they just sat and listened to stories or played the games Nell dreamed up. But pretty soon, Nell discovered that some of the Kids were talented too. Now she had them singing, tap dancing, and playing musical instruments.

Nell paid for Carol to take lessons, and Carol turned out to be one of the most popular Kids. Nell claimed Carol might become the next big child star like Margaret O'Brien, Shirley Temple, or even Nell Aldrich as she was back in 1912. The only one of Nell's Kids who was as good as Carol was Billy DuPree, who could play the xylophone and the harmonica at the same time.

Matthew didn't get to be on the show. Not that he'd wanted to; he would have been the oldest

Shirley Temple

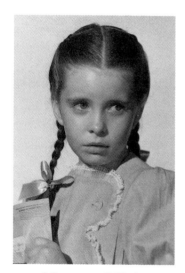

Margaret O'Brien

Aunt Nell's Kid. And he had no talent, except for the guitar, and he wasn't too good on that. He'd asked for an electric guitar on his twelfth birthday but got a plain old acoustic one instead.

That was better than nothing, he figured. He was trying to play by listening to records. Ronnie Green had told him which records to buy. He and Ronnie had kept in touch after the birthday party for Nell and Rocco. Matthew had called Ronnie up because he wanted to know where you could buy an electric guitar. Ronnie met him in the Loop downtown and took him to a music store. The only electric guitar they had cost $200, which was more or less a fortune. You could buy a used Ford for that. It might as well have been $2,000, as far as Matthew was concerned.

But the great thing about the music store was that it sold records. The kind of records Matthew had never heard before. When he listened to one, right there in the store, he felt like he'd opened a window onto a different world. One where the sounds were new, the colors were strange, and nothing would ever seem the same as it was before he went there.

It was hard to explain, and Matthew didn't try. He bought two records in the store and took them home. When he played them on the phonograph in the living room, his mom said that was awfully weird music for him to be listening to.

"It's rhythm and blues," Matthew told her.

"Is that what you call it?" she replied. "Sounds like race music."

"What's race music?" He thought she meant something that people would play at races.

Mom seemed annoyed. "Music that Negroes listen to," she said.

Matthew was surprised. "Just them? Why?"

She shook her head. "Ask your father."

So after supper, as soon as Dad settled into his favorite chair to read the evening newspaper, Matthew approached him.

"Dad?" he said. "Can I ask you something?"

His father looked over the top of the newspaper. "Right now?"

"Well . . . I guess not."

"Oh, all right. Let's get it over with. Is this about school?"

"No."

"Keep your grades up and your head down, that's my advice." Dad laughed. He enjoyed his own jokes.

"It's not school," Matthew repeated. "It's something to do with music Mom told me to ask you."

"Oh. Well, I can tell one note from another, but I'm not really . . ."

"Let me just play this record for you, OK, Dad?"

Dad shrugged. "Sure. What have you got there? Something by Bing Crosby? Patti Page? That new fellow, Tony Bennett?"

Matthew put the thick black record on the turntable and set the tone arm on it. Dad listened to it all the way through. He didn't smile, but he didn't look as angry as Mom had either.

"Where'd you get that?" Dad finally asked.

"At a store. But what I wanted to know—"

"That's race music. They're not selling it around here, are they?"

"No, I got it downtown in the Loop."

Dad nodded. "I would hope not." He laughed again, this time before he'd even told the joke. "If they were selling that kind of record around here, I'd have to go see who the new neighbors were."

Matthew thought about it. "You mean because they'd be colored?"

"Just a joke, son. You wouldn't find coloreds buying a home in Oak Park. Nobody would sell to them, and if they did—"

"But is it OK if I listen to this kind of music?"

"Oh, is that what you wanted to know? Sure, go ahead." Dad thought about it, then added, "I'd rather you didn't play it for your sister, though. It might influence her, and she could have a future as a singer, Nell says."

The next day, Dad brought home a smaller record player for Matthew's room. "It's got three speeds on it," Dad said. "The latest thing."

"What do I need three speeds for?"

"The record companies are introducing slower-speed records so they can get more music on a platter. Probably they'll use them only for long classical works. Which you might want to think about when you outgrow race records."

"Which speed do I use to play the records I already have?"

"At 78."

So whenever Matthew played his records he closed the door to his room and listened by himself. He tried to play along with the records on his guitar, figuring out the chords. Sometimes he got discouraged, because even if he got good at it, he figured nobody would want to listen to him. Meanwhile, his sister was becoming so famous that the kids at Matthew's school pointed him out as "Carol Woods's brother."

Once, Matthew invited Ronnie to come out to listen to records with him. But Ronnie said he didn't want to.

"Why not?" Matthew asked."

"The place where you live–Oak Park?–I'd feel funny out there."

Matthew didn't understand.

"Look," Ronnie said. "How'd you like to come down to 76th Street and listen to records in *our* apartment?"

Matthew didn't know what to say. His parents didn't mind him taking the El train to the Loop by himself, but everybody knew it was dangerous to go to the South Side.

"You see?" Ronnie said. "You'd feel just as funny on my turf."

Matthew didn't feel it was the same thing, but he shrugged. So every so often he and Ronnie

Chicago's South Side

would meet in the Loop and go someplace together. Beside the music store, they went to a shop that sold novelties, magic tricks, and puzzles. Sometimes they went to a movie. But one Saturday, Ronnie asked, "Wanna go see Muddy Waters?"

Muddy Waters was Matthew's favorite singer. Every time he saved a dollar, he would spend it on a Muddy Waters record.

"But," Matthew asked, "how can we ever get to see *him*? He just plays at clubs, right?" And the rhythm-and-blues clubs were only open long after Matthew had to be home in bed.

"He's gonna play at the 708 Club tonight," Ronnie said. "But my dad is going to sit in on piano. And they're gonna rehearse this afternoon. I can get us in."

Matthew hesitated. He was a little afraid. He'd never been that far down on the South Side before. But Ronnie would be with him, and it was a chance to see Muddy Waters. In person. "Sure," he said, as if he did this every day of the week, "let's go."

The club wasn't far from the El tracks, but Matthew was nervous every step of the way. All the other people on the street were colored, and he felt like everybody was looking at him.

They came to the club and went through an alley to the side door. An old man sat on a chair inside reading a newspaper. He hardly glanced up as they went by him.

Matthew and Ronnie stood in the wings of the stage and saw the musicians. The men just seemed to be doodling around and trading jokes. Matthew recognized Ronnie's father, seated at a spinet piano. Next to him was a craggy-faced colored man tuning his guitar. Muddy Waters himself.

"Wanna sit out front?" Ronnie asked as if he owned the club. "We can hear better there."

What Matthew really wanted to do was go up and ask Muddy Waters how he learned to play the guitar like that. And what did he do to get the sound it made when he sang?

But of course, he didn't do that. Instead he went out front with Ronnie. There were some other people at the tables around the club. A couple of the spectators were white, Matthew noticed. So he felt a little less strange, like he wasn't the only white person who liked rhythm and blues.

Ronnie pulled a couple of chairs close to the stage. The boys sat down just as the band started to play. Listening to the music in person was a thousand times better than hearing it on a record. It came right at your face like the cold wind blowing off Lake Michigan in winter. And when Muddy Waters began to sing, Matthew felt like he was hearing music for the first time.

It was too bad that it was a rehearsal because sometimes the band stopped right in the middle of a song. Muddy Waters would tell the rest of the musicians how he wanted something to sound, and then they'd start over.

Matthew watched closely the way Muddy Waters placed his fingers on the neck of the guitar to play chords, and how he plucked at the strings. Matthew's own fingers itched because he wanted to get home and try them out on his guitar.

Muddy Waters

Once, when the band stopped playing, Muddy Waters looked down at the boys as if he'd just noticed them. He walked to the edge of the stage. Without saying anything, he just played something loud and strange. He turned away.

"What was that?" Matthew whispered. "Do you think he doesn't want us sitting here?"

"Naw," said Ronnie. "That's just his way of sayin' hello."

The session went on for a long time, but when it ended Matthew was disappointed. He wanted to hear more. Then he looked at his watch and saw that it was past six. "I gotta go!" he said. "I'll be late for dinner."

Ronnie walked back to the El station with him, but then they headed home in opposite directions. Matthew sat in the El car, looking out at the lights coming on all over the city. All he could think about was Muddy Waters's music. He imagined how it would feel to play it. His fingers moved up and down the strings of an imaginary guitar, and sounds ran through his head. The wheels of the El train beat out a rhythm, and Matthew's head bobbed back and forth. He didn't care if people thought he was crazy or not.

When he came in the front door of his house, Mom called out from the dining room: "Matthew! You're late!" But it wasn't her I'm-really-angry

Chicago El

voice. He was lucky because Dad and Carol had not gotten home yet either.

"I thought nobody would be here for dinner," said Mom. "I made pot roast too. Where were you all this time?"

Matthew shrugged. "Nowhere."

F O U R

Nell's New Kid

CAROL WAS FEELING UNCOMFORTABLE. THE producer of *The Aunt Nell and Huckleberry Show* had decided it was a good idea to make her the Little Princess. That was a role Nell had once played in the silent movies. But the producer—who was Carol's own dad, so she had nobody to turn to for help—made Carol wear a costume with a tiara and wand. Just like the one Nell had worn about a million years ago.

The wand was all right, although it didn't shoot little stars out of the end, the way Carol had hoped. But pretty soon the whole idea got to be really dopey.

53

Everybody started acting differently toward her. On the show, she was always called "The Little Princess." Huckleberry the Clown stopped spraying seltzer on her and instead bowed down when she came on the set. That somehow seemed worse than getting spritzed.

And the other kids on the show stopped being friends with her. They thought she was just a stuck-up little princess. Especially Billy DuPree, who thought he was a better actor than Carol. He said, "If she can be the Little Princess, why can't I be the Little Prince?"

Everybody said she was chosen because her dad ran the show. That wasn't true. It was really Nell who had suggested it to Dad. Nell had some nutty idea that Carol was going to be the new Nell. The only thing was, that kind of act was old-fashioned. Carol knew nobody could really be that goody-goody anymore. This was the modern age.

Nevertheless, the show was a hit and the viewers loved the Little Princess. So popular that Carol had to quit school to practice singing and dancing and all the other little-princessing things. The network hired a tutor for her so that it looked like she was still learning school stuff. But after the tutor found out Carol could already read and write, she just gave Carol books to read.

Carol didn't think she'd miss school, but she did. What she had liked most were her old friends, and now she hardly ever got to see them at all.

Not even Matthew, her own brother. For some odd reason, Dad felt it wasn't a good idea to spend much time with him. It must be those weird records he played. Naturally that just made Carol more eager to listen in whenever she had time off from the show and training to be a little princess.

One day, when Carol arrived at the TV studio, there was a little boy in a wheelchair out beyond the cameras. She thought she knew who he was, and she was right. "That's Dick Aldrich, Harry's son," Aunt Nell whispered to her. "Poor little tyke has polio. The doctors say he won't walk again. I brought him here because he says this is his favorite show."

Carol looked at him, trying not to stare. Everybody knew about polio. Sometimes it affected your legs and you had to wear braces to stand up. Or if it got into your lungs, you had to be in this big iron canister called an iron lung that helped you breathe. Polio could even kill you, and there wasn't any cure for it.

She was curious about something, but was a little embarrassed to ask Nell about it. "Can you, you know, catch it?"

"From him?" Nell frowned. "No, dear. People get it in swimming pools."

They did? Carol had gone swimming last summer without even worrying about it.

"His parents are very upset," Nell said. "I told them I'd look after him for a while."

"Wouldn't he be better off in California?" asked Carol. "It's warmer there."

Nell shook her head. "Well, Harry—let's just say he's too upset to have Dick around just now. Maybe you could go over and say hello to him, after you put your costume on, of course."

Sure, Carol thought. I couldn't just go say hello, I'm your cousin Carol. *Carol* isn't a big deal, but the Little Princess is.

Even so, she went to the dressing room. It took a while because now she had her own makeup artist who made her face look all pink and her eyes big and surprised. When she looked in the mirror, Carol had begun to think that the Little Princess was some strange person she hardly knew.

She went back to the set, and Dick's eyes lit up when he saw her. They looked so bright in comparison to the rest of him, that Carol was afraid he'd have an attack or something.

"Hello, Dick," she said in her sweetest princess voice.

"Are you really the Little Princess?" he asked.

"Yes, I really am," she said, feeling guilty for saying it.

"Can you grant my wishes?"

She thought quickly. "Um, no, that's a job for a good fairy."

"Oh," he said. He seemed really disappointed. But Carol was afraid that if she said yes, he'd ask her to make him all better. That's what she would ask for if she'd been him.

"I've seen you grant wishes on the TV," he said. "The *real* Princess did, anyway."

She couldn't tell him that on the show, it was just an act. One of the Nell's Kids would ask for something like a new toy. The Princess would suddenly appear with it because it came from a box behind the set. Sometimes the Kids wished for something that a sponsor was advertising, like a cup of Yummy-Choc Chocolate Drink. Then Carol would come out carrying the cup of the awful stuff and the Kid would pretend to be overjoyed.

"Well," Carol told Dick, "I'm not able to grant *all* wishes. Tell me what you want and I'll see what I can do."

His eyes brightened again. He struggled to pull himself upright in the chair but couldn't quite make it. She reached out and helped him. It was surprising how little he weighed. "I want," he said, out of breath from the effort, "I want to be one of Aunt Nell's Kids."

"Oh, is that all?" Carol was relieved. "Just a minute." She went over to Mike, the floor director.

"Little Princess," he said, "What can I do for you?"

"See that boy in the wheelchair?" she said. "Can you put him in with Nell's Kids today?"

"Oh, no, sorry," Mike said. "That's a no-no."

She was puzzled. "What's a no-no?"

"Having somebody in the Kids who has something wrong with them. Remember last summer when Jerry broke his arm? We couldn't let him on camera as long as he was wearing a cast."

"But that's dumb," Carol protested.

"It would be even worse if we showed your little friend over there," Mike said. "I mean . . . a wheelchair! He'd frighten the kids who are watching the show at home."

Ashamed, Carol recalled her own first reaction when she saw Dick. But thinking of that only made her more determined. "He is not going to give anybody polio," she said. "Not over the television."

Speaking to her as if she were about five years old, instead of eleven, Mike said, "Look, Princess, I don't make the rules. I just have to follow them. No . . . sick or crippled kids! Got that? Now get ready. Air time is in two minutes."

He turned his back, leaving her clenching and unclenching her fists. If she really did have a magic wand, she knew just what she'd do with it right now.

Slowly, she went back to Dick, who looked at her with those cute little eager eyes. Carol hated to disappoint him. "Look . . . um . . . they've got too many Nell's Kids already," she said.

The shining light in his eyes went out. "Oh."

"Yeah, but . . . be patient," she said. "I'm going to . . . fix it somehow."

"You don't have to," he said. "I understand."

"You do?"

"It's the same way my dad is. He's a movie star."

"Yeah, I know who he is."

"But he's really strong and brave and does all these neat things in real life. He was a race driver and he rides horses and swims . . ." Dick trailed off. "I can't do those things, so he kind of leaves me with Aunt Nell."

"You mean—"

"Because he gets unhappy when he sees me. He tries not to show it, but I can tell. Because I'm not—you know." He gave a little smile.

"Big and strong like him," Carol finished. She was getting really angry now.

"Yes." Dick looked down, and Carol could tell he was trying not to cry.

"Hey," she said. "I'm the Little Princess, right?"

He nodded without looking up.

"Well, stay right here and I'm going to grant you this one wish, anyway. Even if they kick me off the show."

A buzzer sounded, meaning there were only thirty seconds to air time. "I gotta go," she told him "Don't move." Then she thought what a stupid thing to say *that* was.

The music for the show's theme song was starting. Aunt Nell was seated in her rocking chair in the middle of the set. Surrounding her, on the floor, were the Nell's Kids. Carol went over and stood in her place behind Nell's chair. From a glass booth high above the set, Mike gave them the "on-air" signal. On cue, they all began to sing the theme song:

Aunt Nell and Huckleberry
Have lots of fun to carry
Into your house.
Yes, into your *house . . .*

As the show went on, Carol was thinking of the way that day's script was supposed to go. First, Aunt Nell would ask everybody what they'd done lately. Earlier Mike had given all the Kids a piece of paper with the answers they were supposed to give.

Carol, as the Little Princess, had to say she had granted a wish for a little girl who wrote in and asked for a puppy. She really hadn't sent anybody a puppy; it was just a story.

The other kids had stories too—more normal ones like what they did after school. The girls helped their mothers bake pies or sew dresses. The boys hit home runs in baseball games or went exploring in the woods. All these stories were made up too. Three writers sat in a room somewhere and thought up things for the Kids to say.

After that, Nell read some letters from other kids out in televisionland. They told about their adventures or asked for wishes to be granted. Carol suspected most of these letters also came from the show's writers.

Today, however, everybody got a surprise. When Nell turned and said, "Well, Little Princess, tell us what *you've* been doing," Carol responded,

"Aunt Nell, I'm getting ready to grant somebody a wish."

"Oh?" Nell was surprised, but went right on. "Who's that?"

Stepping out of her place behind the chair, Carol said, "Your special guest." She walked across the set to Dick's wheelchair. The camera followed her part of the way, but then stopped. Carol glanced at the camera operator and realized he was getting instructions from Mike through his earphones. Carol was pretty sure she knew what those instructions were.

But that didn't matter. She went to the back of Dick's chair and just wheeled him back onto the set right next to Nell. The show was going out over the air all across America at that moment. If Mike shut it off, the network wouldn't have anything to broadcast. Carol was pretty sure *that* was a bigger no-no than showing a little boy in a wheelchair.

Nell was a trooper, as she had often told Carol. "Well, hello, Dick," she said just as if she had been expecting him. "Kids, let's all say hello to Dick."

"Hellooooo, Dick!" they chorused obediently.

Carol looked up at the glass booth. Mike had his arms folded and was glaring at her. If she had not been on camera, she would have stuck out her tongue. Maybe she should anyway.

Nell had started to chat with Dick, and even though nobody had written a script for him, he seemed to be answering.

"I have a question for Dick," Carol broke in. She figured she was going to get fired after this show, so why not ask what she really wanted to?

"Why, certainly, Princess," said Nell. "What is it?"

Carol took a deep breath. "I hope you don't mind," she said to Dick. However, the look on his face indicated he was having the time of his life. "What I'd like to ask you is . . . how does it feel to have polio?"

It seemed like everybody in the studio had turned to stone. Nobody moved. Nobody made a sound. Carol felt like she'd said maybe the worst thing anybody on television ever had. Radio too.

Dick broke the silence. "You know," he said, "nobody ever asked me that before."

"You don't have to answer," Carol said. "I'm sorry."

"No," he said, shaking his head. "I want to tell."

Up in the booth, Carol saw, Mike just put his head down on his arms and cried.

Even before the show was over, people started to call the network. Carol saw Mike and his assistant answering the phones in the booth. At the commercial break, though, nobody rushed out to wheel Dick off the set.

In fact, while they were off the air, Dick asked for another wish. "Could Huckleberry hit me with one of his custard pies? It always looks like fun."

"Well," said Huckleberry (or Charley) when they told him, "if my career in broadcasting weren't over already, attacking a boy in a wheelchair ought to finish it off nicely." But Dick was having such a good time that Charley did it anyway.

And then came the surprise. The phone calls, as it turned out, were mostly from people who wanted Dick to be on the show *all the time*. "They like him," Mike said after the show was over. He looked dazed. "The switchboard is jammed. We're even starting to get telegrams."

"Carol, that was a great idea," Nell said.

Carol had already thought about that. "Aunt Nell," she said, "you brought him to the studio. I'll bet you knew he wanted to be on the show, didn't you?"

Nell's eyes twinkled as she wagged her finger at Carol. "Maybe so, dear, but it took somebody daring to grant his wish. Only a princess could do that!"

A-Bomb
Drill

RONNIE DIDN'T LIKE HIS MATH TEACHER. THERE wasn't much Ronnie *did* like about junior high school, except the band, but he disliked the math teacher most of all.

Mr. McNamara acted as if teaching here was some kind of punishment. Like he'd been destined for greater things but an evil troll put a curse on him and sent him to Cavanaugh Junior High.

Every day he showed up in the same brown suit and brown shoes and carrying his battered brown briefcase. The only thing that changed was the color of his bow tie. The shirt was always white, and maybe, like the suit, *it* was the same one every day too.

At the beginning of the year, Mr. McNamara had noticed Ronnie smiling. This was a no-no, as far as Mr. McNamara was concerned. He didn't know what Ronnie was smiling about, but he suspected it was something he, Mr. McNamara, had said. And he never made jokes in class.

"I'm keeping an eye on you, mister," said Mr. McNamara. He called all the boys in the class "mister" and all the girls "miss." Bill Monro, who sat next to Ronnie (and who had been the one Ronnie was *really* smiling at) said Mr. McNamara did that because he couldn't remember their names.

Ever since that day, however, Mr. McNamara remembered who Ronnie was. Whenever Ronnie got the least little bit out of line, Mr. McNamara would slap him with a detention. And he took off for "lack of neatness" on Ronnie's homework too.

So Ronnie decided to keep an eye on Mr. McNamara. He began to make a list of his bow ties and the days when he wore them. He kept a sheet of paper on which he marked Mr. McNamara on how well his shoes were shined and how clean his white shirt looked.

A couple of times, when Ronnie was at the blackboard and Mr. McNamara's back was turned, he snuck a look inside the old brown briefcase. That was disappointing. The only thing he saw besides schoolbooks and test sheets were paperback novels of the Wild West.

Today, when Mr. McNamara came to class (a green-and-blue striped bow tie day) he found a message on his desk. He looked at it suspiciously: In the past, some boys had placed rude notes there. But when he examined it, he found that it was an official message from the school principal.

Mr. McNamara read it aloud: "During third period today, there will be an air-raid drill. Teachers should review with students the procedures to be followed in case of a nuclear attack. There will not be an actual nuclear attack, and when the alarm sounds, teachers will caution students not to panic. Instead, students should follow the procedures they would take in case of an actual nuclear attack."

Some nervous giggles and whispered jokes swept around the room when Mr. McNamara finished reading. He gave Ronnie a frozen stare; Ronnie easily put on an innocent and hurt look, since he hadn't said a word. "Does anyone find this drill amusing?" asked Mr. McNamara.

Ronnie was dying to raise his hand, but didn't. Neither did anybody else.

"All right," said Mr. McNamara. "Now let's review the procedures we are to follow in case of a nuclear attack. Who knows the procedures?"

Again, no one raised his or her hand. A few people looked sideways at each other, and then looked quickly away, trying not to giggle.

"This is our first year at Cavanaugh," said Vangie Harris, a girl behind Ronnie.

"But you must have had air-raid drills in elementary school," Mr. McNamara replied.

Absent-mindedly, Ronnie nodded. Mr. McNamara saw him, and pointed. "There! You, mister, demonstrate the procedure for the class."

Ronnie was stunned. Everybody in the front rows turned to look at him. Next to him, Bill Monro said in a quiet, high-pitched voice, "Oooo. Teacher's pet."

"I don't know how, sir," said Ronnie.

"Don't tell me that, mister," said Mr. McNamara. "I saw you nodding. I've got my eye on you."

Ronnie made a face.

"Now go ahead," Mr. McNamara said. "Class, watch this student demonstrate the proper procedure. Imagine that you are hearing the alarm, right now. What's your next move, mister?"

Ronnie remembered what the teachers in elementary school had made them practice. He stood up.

"He's getting out of his seat," announced Mr. McNamara, as if everybody couldn't see that already.

Ronnie squatted down and slid under his desk. "He has positioned himself under the desk," said Mr. McNamara.

Finally Ronnie put his head between his knees and clasped his arms over his head.

"Now, do you all see?" said Mr. McNamara. "He's got his head—"

He stopped because a high-pitched sound was coming from underneath Ronnie's desk: "Eeeeee-eeeeeee."

Air raid drill

It was Ronnie. The high screech turned into moans, and then words: "I'm gonna die! Oh, noooooooo. I'm gonna dieee . . ."

"Stop that!" Mr. McNamara barked. "Come out from under there at once!"

Ronnie didn't move. "Please, please. I don't wanna die."

The rest of the class was breaking up with laughter. Mr. McNamara clapped his hands for order, but nobody paid attention. Ronnie's moans and cries continued.

"All right, mister . . . mister . . ." Mr. McNamara turned to Bill Monro and said, "What's his name, anyway?"

"His name? Ronnie," Bill said. Squealer, thought Ronnie.

"All right, Mister Ronnie," said Mr. McNamara. "If you don't stop this second, you're going straight to the principal's office."

"Eeeeeeeeeeeee, I don't wanna dieee."

The principal was Dr. Clementon, a heavy-set colored woman who wore glasses that hung from a cord around her neck. Nobody knew why, because she never actually put the glasses on her nose and looked through them.

Ronnie had to wait forty-five minutes in the outer office before Dr. Clementon's secretary escorted him in to see her. Waiting was the hardest part. He guessed that was why they made you wait.

When he sat in the chair in front of Dr. Clementon's desk, she made him wait some more. She was writing with a thick black-and-gold fountain pen. When she finished, she carefully put the cap back on the pen and tightened it.

Then, finally, she looked up. Her dark brown eyes didn't show anger or sympathy or anything he could tell. He felt like a mouse in front of a cat.

"Mr. McNamara has reported you for disrupting the nuclear attack alert drill," said Dr. Clementon.

Ronnie didn't say anything. He couldn't think of anything to say except "I don't wanna dieeee," and that probably wouldn't help the situation.

"Do you have anything to say for yourself?"

"No, ma'am," he said.

"Did you think it was funny to disrupt the nuclear attack alert drill?"

"I was . . . sort of demonstrating it," Ronnie explained. "Mr. McNamara asked me to."

"Well," said Dr. Clementon, as if that threw a new light on things, "since he chose you out of the entire class to demonstrate something as serious as that, didn't you feel a sense of responsibility?"

Ronnie took a breath. He wanted to ask Dr. Clementon if she'd seen the pictures of nuclear bomb tests on television. The new ones, with the hydrogen bombs. The scientists built little towns full of houses in the desert and then set off a hydrogen bomb. The movie cameras showed everything getting wiped out, blown away, whole buildings disintegrating in a fraction of a second.

"Do you think anybody could live through that?" he asked.

"I beg your pardon?" Dr. Clementon asked.

Ronnie realized he had spoken out loud. She didn't know what he was talking about. "I meant . . . what good will it do to get under the desk if a hydrogen bomb fell on Chicago?"

Dr. Clementon showed some emotion for the first time. She looked as if Ronnie had insulted her. She picked a sheet of paper from her desk and held it up. "Do you know what this is?"

He started to read the heading, which was in big black print. "Procedures for—"

She snatched it away from his eyes. "This is the Procedure for Conducting a Nuclear Attack Drill."

"Oh," he said.

"And do you know who sent it to this school?"

Ronnie shook his head.

"The United States Government Agency for National Self-Defense in Case of a Nuclear Attack, that's who."

Ronnie nodded.

"Do you think that a government agency would send us *false information*?"

She looked pretty worked up over it, so Ronnie just said, "No, ma'am."

"Of course not," she said, as if she'd just saved him from some horrible fate. "So what you were doing this afternoon was *endangering the lives of every student in the school.*"

There wasn't anything Ronnie could do but hang his head in shame.

"What do you think you should do to make up for that?" asked Dr. Clementon.

Ronnie couldn't really think of anything.

"I want you to write a letter of apology to Mr. McNamara," Dr. Clementon told him.

He nodded. Maybe he could get out of this without too much trouble.

"And," she continued, "you will write an essay of not less than two full pages explaining why we should obey our government."

Two pages, he thought. OK, still not too bad.

"In addition, I want you to bring both the apology and the essay back to my office, with your parents' signatures on them."

Ouch.

"What'd you do at school today, Ronnie?" Mom asked as soon as she heard the front door close.

He knew she'd ask; she always did. So he had an answer ready. "I got chosen for this project."

"Oh, that's great. What kind of project?"

"A writing project. I'm supposed to write an essay and a letter to my teacher."

"You usually don't like to write. Why'd they pick you?"

"There was a contest, and I won."

"Really! I guess you're doing better in junior high than you thought."

"When I'm finished, you and Daddy are supposed to sign the paper, to show you approve of my writing."

"Of course we will. Your daddy will be so proud. Oh, and I almost forgot to tell you . . . that friend of yours called."

"Who? Bill Monro?"

"No, not him. That other boy, you know, the one—"

"Matthew?"

"Yes, that's him. How come he never comes here to see you?"

"Mom, I told you. He's this white kid, lives out in Oak Park."

"Well, that doesn't matter. You could invite him here. We've got nothing to be ashamed of."

"That isn't the point."

"Well, what *is* the point, I'd like to know."

Ronnie couldn't answer. He wasn't sure why he didn't want Matthew coming down here. Maybe Ronnie didn't want him to see the neighborhood, which had pawnshops and storefront churches and places that had illegal gambling in the back. Ronnie knew it wasn't anything like Oak Park. Oak Park was like the places people lived on TV.

But Matthew had invited *him* to come out to Oak Park, and Ronnie hadn't wanted to. Why was that? Was he going to be embarrassed or something?

What was he doing anyway, running around with some dumb white kid? Always asking Ronnie questions about music. It wasn't Matthew's kind of music. Why'd he want to pretend it was?

But Ronnie knew Matthew wasn't pretending. Finally, he dialed the phone and Matthew picked up after two rings.

"Ronnie," he said. "I heard this song. I was in Baker's yesterday, and somebody was playing it."

Oak Park, Chicago

Baker's was the music store in the Loop where Ronnie had taken Matthew. Ronnie felt a little resentful that now Matthew was going there without him.

"You've got to hear it," said Matthew.

"Yeah?"

"Really. It's the coolest."

Ronnie was pretty sure Matthew never said something was cool before Ronnie taught him to. Unless he was talking about a refrigerator. But despite himself, Ronnie was curious. "What's the name of it?"

"Sh-Boom."

"Sh-Boom?" Ronnie started to laugh.

"No, really," Matthew protested. "That's the name."

"All right, OK," Ronnie said. "It's just that it's kind of weird. Somehow it fits into what's been happening to me today."

"What happened?"

"I'll tell you later." Ronnie's mother was listening in the next room, he knew.

"You want to come out and listen to it?" asked Matthew.

"Well, I could just go to Baker's and hear it," Ronnie replied.

"No, they're sold out," Matthew told him. "I bought the last one."

The Chords

Ronnie thought about it for a second. "Sh-Boom," he said again. "Who sings it?"

"A group called the Chords."

"Never heard of them."

"I never did either. Mr. Baker said they're from New York. So you wanna come out and hear it or not?"

Why not? thought Ronnie. "I guess it sounds like something I gotta hear," he said. "Tell me how I get out to your house."

Give It a Chance

JULY 1956

"FACE IT. WE NEED MORE THAN A GUITAR AND drums," Ronnie said.

Matthew agreed. It had taken them more than a year just to save up the money to buy those. It was hard to find jobs when you weren't even sixteen years old yet. You couldn't work as a movie theater usher or bagging in a grocery store. There was a new drive-in restaurant called McDonald's that hired high school kids, but still nobody under sixteen.

Matthew had a newspaper route and Ronnie caddied at the Oak Park Country Club. It was harder for Ronnie because he had to come all the

McDonald's Restaurant

way up from the South Side and give up his weekends. But he actually made more than Matthew because the golfers gave him good tips.

Neither of them enjoyed their jobs. Matthew always had phone calls complaining that he hadn't left the newspaper in the right place, or that the newspaper got wet because he tossed it near the lawn sprinkler, or that a dog had chewed it up. And it was tough collecting the money from some people too.

As for Ronnie, caddying at a whites-only country club was like being condemned to carry Mr. McNamara's briefcase wherever he went. And smile while he was doing it. Ronnie found out that the more he smiled, the bigger his tips were. One Sunday night after he got home, Ronnie's mother asked him how come he was smiling so much. He hadn't realized he was still doing it.

The two of them had worked hard because they wanted to start a band. Maybe it was when they first listened to "Sh-Boom," or maybe it was when other singers followed the Chords in making records with that kind of music. Maybe it was when station WOPA started to play those records all the time. Now you didn't even have to buy them to listen.

Matthew and Ronnie still bought a lot of them even so. The three-speed record player that Matthew's dad had bought him came in handy, because the stores were selling the new records that played at 45 speed. For some odd reason, the 45s had a big hole in the center. You had to buy a plastic thing that fit into the big hole and let you slip it onto one of the old thin-spindle record players.

When the two boys started listening, they were the only two kids they knew who liked this kind of music. Not anymore. And it wasn't called race music or rhythm-and-blues music either. The disk jockeys

Ronnie

who played it on the radio called it rock and roll.

Maybe that was the moment when Matthew and Ronnie decided to start a band—when they realized that everybody their age was listening to this music.

Older people still didn't get it. After Matthew had played Chuck Berry's song "Maybelline" over and over one day, his mom burst into his room. She told him if he played it *one more time,* she'd shut off that record player for good.

Matthew was amazed. He hadn't been aware that his mom could even hear the record. He knew that she didn't much like the rhythm-and-blues records, but they didn't send her up the wall the way "Maybelline" did.

In fact, the more the kids listened to rock and roll, the less the older people liked it. The *Chicago Tribune* ran articles that called it "an unhealthy obsession of reckless American youth." Ministers began to attack it as "the devil's music." Some people said it could destroy the moral fiber of anyone who listened to it.

Matthew couldn't figure it out. Whenever *he* listened to it, he didn't feel any of those things. It just made him feel good.

At school, kids knew the words to all the latest songs and tried to sing them at lunch hour. People started to tap out the beat on the lunch tables. All this drove the lunchroom monitors crazy. The principal banned anyone from singing or playing rock-and-roll songs.

The same thing was happening at Ronnie's school, and just about every other school in the country. The older people kept worrying about the mysterious hold the music had on teen-

Matthew

agers. And teenagers wondered—when they weren't dancing or listening to it—why the older people didn't like it as much as they did.

Matthew and Ronnie decided that the best place to practice playing rock and roll was in Matthew's garage. Dad's car was gone during the day and Mom parked hers in the driveway. Even so, Matthew figured it was going to be tough to persuade Mom to let him and Ronnie use the garage.

She surprised him again. He guessed it was because he asked if she'd mind if he and Ronnie listened to records in the garage.

"You mean you're going to move the record player out there?"

"Yeah, kinda. I mean, I'll make sure it doesn't get dirty or anything . . ."

"Go right ahead," she said. "The farther away from the house, the better."

"Um . . . we might play our own music along with it. Just to see if we can."

"Anything. Only shut the garage door so the neighbors don't complain."

Mom's idea was actually pretty good. With the door shut, they got a really neat echo chamber effect and the music sounded even louder.

For a while it was fun just playing along with the records, seeing if they could keep in tune. But Matthew and Ronnie realized that they were going to need more musicians.

"There's another thing," said Ronnie. "You sing like a wounded owl."

"Yeah, well you're pretty terrible yourself."

Ronnie nodded. "We can do the doo-wop backgrounds, but we need a lead singer with a good voice."

"How about me?"

They both jumped in surprise and looked up. In the rafters of the garage was a platform where some old trunks and boxes of junk were stored. Peering over the edge was Matthew's sister Carol.

"What are you doing up there?" Matthew asked angrily. She had scared him.

"Listening to you guys. You're not too bad, but you're right. You need a singer and a couple more instruments. Like I said, how about me?"

"You? For what?"

"A singer. I happen to sing on television, in case nobody's let you in on the secret."

"That isn't the kind of singing we need. We're going to play rock and roll."

"Hey, I know that. I can sing that."

"You can't. You just sing those dumb Mary Had a Little Lamb songs."

"I'm tired of that," she said. "Nobody wants to admit it, but I'm too old for it. You know what? When Nell was in the silent movies, she was playing little-girl roles till she was over twenty! I'm not getting caught in that trap."

Matthew looked at his sister. Sometime in the last year or so, she'd grown up. They still curled her hair and dressed her like a princess on the TV show. Without all that, she looked more like a person. But singing for a rock-and-roll band—*his* rock-and-roll band—he didn't think so.

"Girls can't sing rock and roll," he said.

"*I* can," she replied.

"Like what?"

"I can sing 'Heartbreak Hotel.'"

Matthew tried not to look impressed. He glanced at Ronnie. "Only Elvis sings that," said Ronnie.

"I heard the two of you try to play it," Carol said. That was true. It was one of the songs they couldn't sing.

"Anyway," said Carol casually, "I met Elvis."

Elvis Presley

The boys couldn't help gawking at her. "You did not. Don't lie to us."

"I did," she insisted. "Somebody at the studio got me a ticket when he was on *The Milton Berle Show*. And because they knew who I was, they let me backstage. I got his autograph."

"Aw, let's hear you sing it," said Ronnie. Matthew played a chord on the guitar, and Carol launched into the song. She wasn't as good as Elvis—who was?—but she was pretty much all right. Lots better than the boys had thought she'd be.

"OK, OK," Matthew said when she'd finished. "How'd you learn to sing that way?"

"I started by listening to you play those records," she said.

"Oh. Well, don't tell Dad that, all right?"

The next weekend, the band had more members. When Ronnie's sister Michelle learned what was happening, she insisted on coming too. "She plays the saxophone pretty good," Ronnie explained to Matthew.

Michelle

Matthew could hardly object. His own sister had brought another of the Nell's Kids, Billy DuPree. "He's kind of a big pain," Carol whispered to Matthew. "But he can really play the xylophone, and the harmonica too."

"He didn't *bring* the xylophone," Matthew pointed out.

"It's on the way," said Carol. "I talked a couple of the stagehands into carting it here from the TV studio. They have a truck."

That made Matthew a little nervous. "Carol, what's Dad going to say if he finds out?"

She shrugged. "What can he say?"

"He can kill me, first. I know he's not going to like you singing in the band."

"I'll fix it up with Nell," Carol said confidently. Matthew didn't feel so confident.

The xylophone did arrive, and the two stagehands decided to stay for what they called the rehearsal. They had to take the xylophone back to the studio that night anyway.

Matthew was relieved. At least Dad wouldn't come home and find a xylophone where he wanted to park his car.

However, he wasn't sure just what they were going to rehearse. The band had trouble keeping in time with each other, even when they were playing along with a record.

Billy DuPree

Everybody realized it too. Ronnie started to look bored, and Matthew worried that he might pack up and leave any minute.

Finally Carol called a halt. "Look, you guys," she said, "I thought you wanted to start a *band*."

"We were doing OK till you came along," Ronnie grumbled.

Carol ignored that. "The trouble is, we're playing along with records. We're trying to imitate somebody else."

"Yeah, well where else are we going to get songs to play?" asked Ronnie.

Carol shot a smile in Billy DuPree's direction. "I guess he never watches Aunt Nell and Huckleberry, does he?"

"That's a dumb baby show," said Ronnie.

"Well, here's how we build songs there," Carol shot back.

"I'm not playin' any of that candy cane music," said Ronnie. "I'm splittin'." He started to get up, but Carol said. "Give it a chance. What have you got to lose?"

Carol

Ronnie hesitated, but then *his* sister imitated Carol's voice on the saxophone: "Give it a chance." Ronnie laughed and sat down. "OK," he said, "I'll give it a chance. What do you want me to do?"

"Just start laying down a nice strong beat," she said. "Like this: ta-da, ta-da, ta-DA."

After Ronnie's drum rhythm took hold, Carol said, "All right, Billy. Follow him on the xylophone. Da-da-da-DOO."

She turned to Matthew. "Did you hear what Michelle just played on the saxophone?"

"Yeah."

"Can you do the same thing on your guitar?"

"I think so." He listened to the melody Michelle was repeating now, and found the key.

Carol let them go on for a couple of bars, while she kept time with a tambourine. Then she turned and started to sing:

Give it a chance
Give it a chance
Go to the dance
Find some romance . . .
What have you got to lose?
Oh oh oh.

Everybody laughed, but they kept on playing because it sounded cool. Carol hadn't thought up the rest of the words yet, so they just repeated the first verse. Then she told Matthew and Ronnie to come up with a background vocal, like de-boppity-bop-bop. "And sing it nice and deep."

Each time through, the song seemed to get a little better. Matthew could hardly believe it. He looked back at Ronnie, who shook his head. But he was smiling. Something had happened. Matthew saw that the stagehands were clapping in time to the music.

Maybe there was still a lot of practicing to be done, and a lot of other obstacles to get by too, but Matthew knew right then they could really have a band. At least that was the story he told whenever he was interviewed about it in years to come.

SEVEN

Play It Loud

AUGUST 1956

"NO," SAID MATTHEW'S DAD. "ABSOLUTELY NOT. I'm putting my foot down. I mean it."

He was the first obstacle. Matthew just hadn't expected to have to face it this soon. But after a couple more weeks of rehearsal, Carol had decided the band was ready.

"We need a catchy name," she said. "That's important."

"A lot of the groups have birds' names," said Michelle. "The Robins, the Flamingoes, the Pelicans."

"No, we want to stand out, have a name that says who we are."

"The Princess and the Paupers," suggested Ronnie with a little crash on his cymbal.

"I'm *not* going to be the Princess anymore," Carol said firmly.

Ronnie shrugged. "Be a big draw. People would like to see the Princess from TV. All of a sudden she's singin' rock and roll."

"How about the Greenwoods?" suggested Matthew.

"Greenwoods?"

"Sure. Ronnie and Michelle's last name is Green. Carol's and mine is Woods. Just put them together."

"How about *me*?" Billy DuPree objected.

"Listen, the name's no big thing," said Ronnie. "Call it whatever you want."

Matthew misunderstood. "What?" he said. "Whatever You Want?"

"No," said Carol. "It needs to be short. We'll be the Whatevers. People will remember that."

"The Whatevers," said Ronnie, trying it out. He laughed. "I like it."

"You guys get to work writing a song with the word *whatever* in it," Carol said. "I'll see if I can get somebody to cut us a record."

"We can't cut a record yet," Ronnie objected. "We're a long way from being ready."

"You can over-rehearse," Carol told him. "Then you lose the fresh sound."

Ronnie turned to Matthew. "This is because you brought your kid sister into this."

Matthew wanted to point out that *Ronnie* had his kid sister in the group too. But he fought back any angry words. "You said we needed a singer." But like Ronnie, Matthew was afraid Carol was running the band now.

Carol made good on her promise, however. She found a company that agreed to let them make a record. "I let them think it had something to do with *The Aunt Nell and Huckleberry Show,*" she admitted to Matthew.

"Well, what's going to happen when they find out it doesn't?" he asked.

"We'll worry about that later."

But they had to worry that same night. The owner of the record company had called Dad.

Naturally he blamed Matthew.

"I want you to get all that junk out of the garage," Dad said. "Tell those friends of yours to keep away from here. And get rid of those records too."

"It's not *his* fault," said Carol. "I want to do this."

That was when Dad said "Absolutely not" and the rest of it.

But *then* . . . Carol said, "OK, the Little Princess just died." She went upstairs to her room and shut the door.

Having nobody else around, Dad glared at Matthew. "Honest, Dad," said Matthew, "I just wanted to play some rock and roll with Ronnie."

"Rock and roll is just a fad," said Dad. "And Carol will calm down by the time supper is on the table."

But she didn't. She was on strike. Mom brought meals upstairs to her, but she wouldn't leave her room. On the TV show, Aunt Nell had to announce that the Little Princess had been kidnapped by trolls. Huckleberry and the other Nell's Kids spent a lot of time trying to rescue her.

Matthew watched the show every day. There wasn't much else to do since he was forbidden to play his records or his guitar. At first the search for Carol was pretty exciting. Nell asked the audience to send in suggestions as to where the Kids should search for the Princess. Matthew figured he could win the prize because he knew exactly where she was.

At the end of a week, Nell came to their house. Not as part of the show—in real life, in a Cadillac limousine driven by a very old man who looked like he came out of a horror movie.

When Mom opened the front door, half the people in the neighborhood were out on their lawns pretending to do something so they could get a look at the TV star and her chauffeur. "What a nice surprise," Mom said. "Would you like some iced tea?"

"I came to see my Princess," Nell said.

"I don't know–" Mom began.

"I do," said Nell. "I know all about it. Where's her room?"

Matthew showed her up the stairs. Nell knocked on Carol's door.

"Go away," came Carol's muffled voice.

"I'm staying till you let me in," Nell replied. "And I was fourteen once too. I can be just as stubborn as you are."

A long silence. Then a click as the door was opened. Carol stood there. "Maybe we can make a deal," she said. Nell went inside and Carol winked at Matthew before she closed the door again.

He finally got tired of standing in the hall trying to hear what they were saying, and went back downstairs. Mom was peeking through the drapes watching the neighbors watching the house. "Carol let Aunt Nell in," Matthew told her.

"Your father says that even though Nell has that sweet air about her, she always gets her way in the end," Mom said.

Just like Carol, thought Matthew. Wonder which one is more stubborn.

After a while, the bedroom door opened Carol and Aunt Nell came down the stairs arm in arm.

Mom looked happy. "I made some cookies," she said. "Chocolate chip, Carol–your favorite kind."

"We'd like some," said Nell.

"Milk?" Mom asked. Nell nodded.

When Mom went to the kitchen, Nell turned to Matthew. "Can you have all the members of this band of yours at the WCBN-TV studios tomorrow afternoon?"

"I think so," he said. "Would they—I mean, should we bring our instruments?"

"Yes," Carol told him. "Aunt Nell is going to give us an audition."

Matthew couldn't believe what he heard. "An audition?"

"Yes, she wants to see our act."

"But we haven't got any—" He thought of all the things they didn't have: an act, enough songs, any experience at all. "Look," he said, "we're not the kind of band she could put on the Aunt Nell show."

"I know that, silly," said Carol. "But if Aunt Nell thinks we're good enough, she'll get us a booking on some other show. Maybe Ed Sullivan."

Ed Sullivan was the host of one of the most popular variety shows on television. Each Sunday night, he presented acts of all kinds—from musical groups to animal trainers to jugglers. Anybody who appeared there, before an audience of millions, became instantly famous. Of course, a lot of them had been famous before the show too.

"But we haven't even . . ." Matthew said. "Nobody knows who we are."

The Ed Sullivan Show

"Ed owes me a few favors," said Nell. "I gave him some tidbits when he was writing a newspaper column."

"It would be our big chance," Carol pointed out to Matthew.

"And don't forget our agreement," Nell said softly.

Carol nodded.

"What agreement?" asked Matthew.

"I told Nell that I'd keep on being the Little Princess for another year and use another name when I'm singing with the Whatevers."

"What name?"

"Carol Lee."

When Matthew called Ronnie to tell him the news, Ronnie was puzzled too. "Let me get this straight," he said. "We're gonna play our songs for this old lady? How old is she?"

"I don't know . . . fifty-six or fifty-seven."

"She's never gonna dig us. Everybody her age hates rock and roll. Even my dad doesn't like it, and he likes rhythm and blues."

"I know, I know," Matthew said.

"She's not gonna try to get us to play baby songs like they have on that show, is she?"

"We don't even know how," Matthew pointed out.

"Maybe she's just sayin' she'll do this because she wants your sister back on her show."

"That *is* why she's doing it."

"But I mean she'll just say thanks, fellas, but you're not good enough. Then what?"

Matthew thought. "I don't know." Then he laughed a little. "But it's like our song."

"What song?"

"Give It a Chance."

When they got to the studio, Matthew's dad was there, looking very agitated. He came up to Matthew. "Was this your idea?" he asked.

Matthew shook his head. "Nell and Carol worked it out by themselves."

"Can't you just tell Carol she can't be in this band of yours? That will solve everything."

Matthew looked at Ronnie. Ronnie said, "Mr. Woods, it wasn't our idea to put her in the band. It was *her* idea."

"Oh, what do *you* know?" said Matthew's dad, and went off to find somebody else.

He had arranged for the audition to take place in a locked soundstage. Nobody was allowed in except the band, himself, and Nell. "Maybe we can just get this over with and put it behind us," Matthew's dad muttered as he let Nell inside and locked the doors.

Hearing that, Matthew worried that Ronnie might be right—this was just going to be a sham—something that would get Carol back on the TV show by convincing her that the band wasn't any good.

"Billy!" Nell said as she walked toward the stage. "Billy DuPree. You're in this band too?"

Billy looked embarrassed, but he rolled his xylophone into place and said, "Yes, Auntie Nell. But you'll like it really."

"How many songs do you want to hear?" Matthew asked Nell.

"Just start with your best one and I'll see if I need to hear more," she said. She took a seat in the front row. Dad tried to sit down too, but he kept popping up and walking up the aisle. Probably he was checking to see if anybody was listening at the door.

Matthew turned to Ronnie. "One song," he repeated.

Ronnie shrugged. "Let's make it Carol's favorite," he said.

"OK, everybody," Matthew said. "'Give It a Chance' it's going to be."

"Make it loud," said Carol.

Matthew stared at her. Loud was probably the last thing that would impress Nell. But he turned up the volume on his amplifier. Carol knew what she wanted.

He played a chord on his guitar, and Carol stepped up to the microphone.

"Give it a chance . . ." she began.

They had written two more verses to the song. By the time the band got to the second one, Matthew was enjoying himself. He forgot about Aunt Nell sitting in judgment in the front row; even forgot about Dad roaming the theater like an unfriendly watchdog.

Matthew was into the music. He was playing it because he liked it, and for no other reason. Liked every part of it. It was his music. It belonged to him and his friends. They knew what it was all about, and if Nell didn't, if Mom and

Dad didn't, or if nobody else in the world did—it didn't matter.

He closed his eyes before the song ended, wanting to enjoy the last echoes of the music as long as he could.

Then his dad's voice broke the spell. "OK, is that it? That's all, then. Wrap it up. Let's get out of here."

Matthew opened his eyes. For some reason he looked down at Nell. At least she didn't look like somebody had struck her with an ax. In fact . . .

"Just a minute, Freddy," she said. "I'd like to hear another."

"Another?" said Dad, as if she'd asked for another jolt from the electric chair.

"Yes, I wonder if it all sounds alike, as people say."

Carol turned to face the band. "Let's play 'Whatever You Want.'"

That was really pushing their luck. Matthew and Ronnie had just finished the song the day before Dad found out about the band. They had only played it once.

"Why not 'Heartbreak Hotel'?" Matthew suggested. "You sing that great."

"But it's not *our* song," she said. "Elvis made it famous. 'Whatever You Want' is ours."

"Go ahead, Matthew," Ronnie called out.

Matthew nodded. The new song was softer than "Give It a Chance." Nell wouldn't think it sounded the same. He hoped. He started to play, and Carol sang:

Whatever you want
Whatever you want
I will give you
Whenever you hurt
Whenever you hurt
I will heal you
Wherever you go
Wherever you go
I will be there.
Be there, be there
For you

Matthew had helped write the words, but when his sister sang them, she turned them into something different, something a real girl would sing. Not that Carol wasn't real, but she was his sister. Aw, well, he told himself, might as well not think about it. Just play.

This time when the song was over, there was no doubt about Nell's reaction. She clapped. Dad just shook his head and ran his fingers through what was left of his hair.

"I wondered what all the fuss was about with this rock and roll music," said Nell. "Now I think I understand. Of course, we couldn't play it on *my* show . . ." Dad rolled his eyes just at the thought of it. ". . . but I see why all the young people like to dance to it."

Ronnie played a rat-a-tat on his snare drum.

"You need a little more practice," said Nell. "And I think before you go on television, you might want to bring out a record or two. Like that Elvis boy."

Matthew exchanged glances with Ronnie. A record! They tried not to grin too much at the thought of it. Matthew imagined himself going into Baker's music store and seeing his record on the shelves. Maybe even hearing it played over the store's sound system as a featured record.

"I just have one question," Nell said.

Matthew tensed up. What would this be? Did she want them to sing some other song? Drop somebody from the band?

But it was neither of those. She asked, "Did you play so loud because you thought I couldn't hear?"

EIGHT

On Stage

IT WAS HARDER THAN THEY THOUGHT IT WOULD be. Not that it was Nell's fault. She sent them to a recording studio in Chicago. She paid for a producer to help them make the record sound as good as possible.

The trouble was, the producer's idea of what was good was different from theirs. A lot different.

"You need more sound," he said after listening to them once. His name was Bernard Bleeck. "Call me Bernie," he told them. He was short, round, and wore a toupee that was a lot darker than it should have been.

"More sound? You want it *louder?*" asked Ronnie. Nobody as old as Bernie had ever wanted them to play louder.

"No, no," Bernie replied. "More . . . texture. More sounds for the ear to play with."

He meant more instruments in the band. Violins and trumpets and trombones. He brought in some older musicians to play them.

Matthew tried to protest. "We don't need more musicians," he told Bernie. "We can't play with them."

"Don't worry," said Bernie. "I'll teach you."

"We're not going to pay for them," said Carol.

"No, don't worry about that," said Bernie. "Your Aunt Nell is paying."

"Not *my* Aunt Nell," grumbled Ronnie.

They tried it, playing "Give It a Chance" with violins and trumpets and trombones. It sounded terrible.

Bernie was pleased, however. "Better," he said. "Now we should do something about the voice."

"The voice?" Carol repeated. "*My* voice?"

"Yes. But don't worry. We can fix it. We'll tape it and overdub five or six times. If that doesn't work, we'll bring in a professional. She'll sing for the record session. When you go on tour, you can just move your lips and *pretend* you're singing . . ."

Carol put up her hand to stop him. He *didn't* stop, but she wasn't listening to him. "Guys," she said, turning to Matthew and the others, "is this what we want?"

They shook their heads.

Carol turned back to Bernie. He was still explaining how she could pantomime someone else's singing. "Bernie," she said, "you're fired."

It took a couple seconds for her words to have an effect, and Bernie kept talking. He was like a windup toy that kept churning its engine even after you flipped it over. "What?" he said.

"I said you're fired. We don't want your help here."

Bernie took a deep breath. A *very* deep breath. Matthew wondered if Bernie were going to explode. He looked like a balloon filling up with air so that its skin got thinner and thinner.

Finally Bernie laughed, but it was more like a shout that came out in spurts. "You can't fire *me.* Do you know who I am?"

"I'm sorry," Carol said.

"I'm Bernie Bleeck!" he said, just in case they hadn't heard. "I have produced forty-seven hit recordings. I produced Perry Como! Patti Page! Vaughan Monroe!"

He drew himself up to his full height, which, after all, was nearly three inches taller

Perry Como   Patti Page

than Carol. "You can't fire *me!*" he shouted. "I fire *you!*"

Carol looked at the rest of the band. "Guess we're fired, then," said Ronnie, picking up his drumsticks.

Matthew's heart sank. He was still dreaming about what it would be like to hear himself on a record. But he knew playing the songs Bernie's way wasn't going to make it happen. He unplugged his guitar.

"Where are you going?" asked Bernie.

"Back to our garage," said Carol.

"Oh, yes?" Bernie said. "Take your little rock-and-roll songs with you. Because a garage is where they belong. It's not going to last, you hear me? In a year or two, even the teenagers will get tired of rock and roll. It's just a fad, like those Davy Crockett coonskin caps. And *then* you'll be sorry you didn't let me show you how to play *real* music."

It took them a while to pack up their instruments. Bernie and the other musicians left before they did. The only one left, besides the band, was a sound engineer in a glass booth.

"You guys leaving too?" he called through a loudspeaker. "You've still got two hours of studio time paid for."

"We do?" Carol said. "Can you record us?"

"Sure, I've been sitting here for three days waiting to push the buttons."

"OK, guys want to try it again?" Carol asked.

"The way we want to do it," said Ronnie.

"Now that nobody's here to tell us we're no good," she added.

So they set up once more. "Let's make it our best," Carol said.

They played both songs. One of them they made a couple of false starts on, but the third time everybody agreed it was just they way they wanted. The second song, "Whatever You Want," went just right on the first take. When it was over, they all waited, thinking Bernie was going to rush out and scream how terrible it was. But nobody said anything. Somehow, they wished they'd had an audience, even Bernie.

Carol looked up at the sound engineer and asked, "How was that? Should we try it again?"

He shrugged. "I don't think you'll do it any better than that."

They laughed.

So they had a tape. But when the head of the record company heard it, he didn't want to release it as a record. "Actually," said Matthew's dad, "he didn't listen to it at all."

"But how could he tell if it was any good or not?" asked Matthew.

"He agreed to distribute the record only because he knew Bernie Bleeck was producing it. So what do *you* do? You lip off to Bernie, refuse to take his advice, and insult him. So he quits." Dad tapped his forehead. "Very smart of you. Very smart."

Matthew had already explained to Dad what really happened. But Dad had said, "Don't blame your sister for it. She's too smart a kid to talk to anybody important that way."

When Matthew met the rest of the band, he told them the bad news.

"But we've still got the tape, right?" asked Ronnie.

"Yeah, it's ours."

"So we can take it to another record company."

Matthew turned to Carol. "What about that? Do you think Nell will help us?"

"I don't know," Carol said. "Bernie happened to be a good friend of hers. She told me we ought to apologize to him, get him to help us some more."

"Can she still get us on *The Ed Sullivan Show*?"

"Ed's decided to put Elvis Presley on instead, and he doesn't want another rock-and-roll act this year."

"Yeah," said Ronnie. "Elvis has only sold about 20 million more records than we have."

Matthew sat down and picked up his guitar. He plucked at the strings half-heartedly. "So we're back where we started," he said. "Maybe it was dumb to think we could ever be a real band."

"Don't talk like that," said Carol. "We *are* a real band. We just need to get the right people to listen to us. Look, you and Ronnie call up some record companies and ask them to listen to the tape. They've got to at least *listen* because they don't know where the next hit is going to come from."

"We can do that," said Ronnie.

"And I'll find some place where we can actually stand up and sing!" Carol said. "What we need most of all is to hear some applause."

Matthew doubted they'd ever hear it, but two days later Carol called him on the telephone from the TV studio. "I found a place that needs a band for this Friday and Saturday night."

"You did? Where is it?"

"Up across the state line in Wisconsin. It's not far. But look, there are a couple of things to remember."

"What?"

"First of all, don't tell Dad. He's going to New York this weekend on business. So we don't want him to worry."

"Why would he worry?"

"You know him. He always worries unless I'm being the Little Princess. Anyway, he'll never find out. But the second thing is important. You've got to tell Ronnie and Michelle. I'll tell Billy."

"Which is?"

"Officially, we're all sixteen."

Matthew didn't say anything for a moment. "Sixteen years old?" he finally blurted out.

"Sure, what'd you think?"

"Look, Carol, I'm the only one who's sixteen. And nobody would ever believe you and Michelle are sixteen."

"They could," said Carol. "We'll wear makeup. Anyway, after we get there, nobody is going to object. I'm just telling you, so you know. Billy and I have child entertainer's permits, but I think they're only good in Illinois. But Michelle doesn't, and Ronnie is still fifteen, right?"

"Right."

"Pass the word on. I gotta go be the Princess now. Don't worry. This is going to be great. I know it." She hung up.

Matthew certainly wasn't sure things were going to be great. And he knew just who was going to be blamed if things went wrong. For the next three days, all he did was worry and imagine terrible things that could happen. He woke up at night from dreams about people booking the band. Once he dreamed he was on stage and looked down to find out he was playing a pineapple instead of a guitar.

But even in his worst dreams, Matthew hadn't imagined how bad the place where they were going to play really was.

Carol hired a limousine to drive them up. The two stagehands brought their instruments in a truck. When they drove into the parking lot, Matthew looked out and saw motorcycles. Lots of them. In fact, a couple more pulled in right behind their limousine. Each of them carried a large, beefy man in a leather jacket and a thin woman in pedal-pushers hanging on behind.

"Carol," Matthew said. "This can't be the right place."

"Sure it is," she said, pointing to the neon sign: BOB'S DEW DROP INN.

Matthew struggled to speak. "This is a . . . a biker bar. It's for motorcycle gangs."

"What's the difference how they get here as long as they like our music?"

For a second, Matthew didn't think he would get out of the car. He looked at Ronnie, who shrugged and said, "Can't be any worse than the Oak Park Country Club." When Matthew's face fell, Ronnie poked him and said, "That's a joke, son."

Some joke, thought Matthew. But he followed the rest of them toward the building.

A big man at the door stopped them. "Huh-uh," he said. "No minors."

"We're the band," said Carol.

He looked them over. "I gotta find Bob," he said. "Wait here."

Bob turned out to be the only skinny-looking man in the place. He even had a thin mustache, and wore suspenders because he was too thin for a belt. "*You're* the Whatevers?" he said when he saw them. "The person I talked to said you had experience. You guys look like you're still in grade school."

"We're not here to drink beer," said Carol. "We're here to play. It's too late for you to get any-body else, so why not give us a try?"

"Thing is," said Bob, "if you're no good, this crowd will get ugly. I'd be better off just making it a free jukebox night." He paused. "You kids could even get hurt."

"We'll take our chances," said Carol.

"Yeah, well, right behind the bandstand there's a door that leads outside. If anybody jumps onto the stage, you go out that door. Understand?"

The first thing Matthew did after they got inside was to find that door and check to make sure it wasn't locked.

The second thing he did was to sneak a look at the audience. They weren't paying attention to him, which he felt was a good thing. The room was dark and smoky so nobody could see how young the band was, he figured.

It took them a while to set up. In the meantime, more people came into Bob's. The sound of everybody talking was so loud that Matthew started to hope it would drown out the music.

Suddenly Bob appeared next to him. "You ready?" he asked, looking at his watch. "Let's get this show on the road."

"Yeah, I guess," said Matthew. He took a look at Carol and Ronnie. Even they seemed to be a little scared, and Matthew realized it was really time. He fought off an urge to head for the door behind the stage.

Bob stepped up to the microphone—a little too close, because it let out a feedback squeal. The loudspeaker was right next to Matthew and he put his fingers in his ears. Bob tapped the microphone, making loud thumps, and said, "Good evening and welcome to another night of fun and games at

Bob's Dew Drop Inn. Give a big hand now for one of the newest and best of the rock-and-roll bands—the Whatevers!"

Nobody in the audience paid the slightest attention, even when Bob was speaking. They went right on talking loudly and slurping their beers. With a flourish of his hand, Bob gave the stage to the band.

Matthew swallowed hard. He looked at the others. "Just pretend we're in our garage," he said. Maybe that was the right way to get through this. If the audience didn't pay any attention, at least they wouldn't jump on the stage.

"Let's start with 'Heartbreak Hotel,'" he said. "They probably like Elvis."

Carol shook her head. "No, let's try the new song. It has a good beat." They had written it last week, but hadn't played it for anyone.

"It's too . . ." Matthew didn't know the right word. "They might turn ugly."

"I don't care," said Carol. "Give me the key."

Checking to see how far the exit door was, Matthew played the song's intro. Carol started to sing:

It doesn't matter
What you want
It doesn't matter
What you say.
That's how I'll play.
It doesn't matter

What you do
'Cause I don't give
A hoot about you.
That's how I'll play.

Once more, Carol transformed the words as she sang them. She turned the song into a taunt that she threw at the audience, daring them to listen.

I'll play the music
I'll sing my song
Any way I want
Even if I'm wrong
That's how I'll play.

People were starting to look up at the stage. Gradually the conversation died down so that all Matthew could hear was the music. His hands started to sweat, and slipped a couple of times on the guitar strings. He thought they reached the end of the song, but Carol was into it, and began to sing the first verse again. The rest of the band just followed her lead.

Matthew heard some noises and peered out into the smoky room. A few people had started to dance. At least, it looked like dancing. They weren't headed toward the stage, at any rate.

Finally, with a loud chord, the song came to an end. The audience started to yell. Matthew took a step back. He couldn't understand whether they were angry or not. Then he heard whistles, and it dawned on him.

They liked us.

A Big Chance

DECEMBER 1956

BY THE TIME THE WHATEVERS HAD FINISHED THEIR first night's work, Bob had a contract for them all to sign. Carol told them to wait until they had a lawyer read it. That was fortunate, for in addition to having the band play at the Dew Drop Inn for a year, Bob wanted to become their agent and take 50 percent of everything they earned.

The lawyer they went to was Ronnie and Michelle's Aunt Lorraine. After talking with her, they all decided they trusted her. "I'm not really an entertainment lawyer," she said, "But I know enough to tell you not to sign this contract."

"We like playing at Bob's, though," said Matthew. "We want to keep doing it."

"Not for the rest of your lives," Lorraine said. "Things move fast in the music business. You guys could become too big for Bob's Dew Drop Inn."

Lorraine fixed up the contract so that they only had to play at Bob's as long as they didn't get a better offer. Matthew figured Bob would be upset when he saw the new contract, but he wasn't.

"Hey," Bob said, offering to shake hands, "I just thought you kids needed a little help getting to the top."

So they went on playing at Bob's every Friday and Saturday. Matthew realized that the experience was making them a better band. They learned how an audience reacted to their music. And whenever the band started to feel discouraged, applause lifted them up again.

The band was good for Bob's Dew Drop Inn, too. The parking lot was hardly big enough to hold all the motorcycles. Even people with cars started to come as word of the band's popularity got around.

Bob put up posters along the highway and took out newspaper ads. Those caused a little argument in the band because they read:

The Whatevers

with

CAROL LEE

appearing Friday
and Saturday nites
at
Bob's Dew Drop Inn
Highway 11
Delavan, Wisconsin

"Ahh, not that I'm complaining," said Ronnie as he showed the ad to the others, "but how'd we get to be The Whatevers with Carol Lee?"

"I didn't even know Bob was going to do that," said Carol. "Tell him to cut it out."

But when they confronted Bob, he explained. "Look, no offense to the rest of you guys, but the little lady is the star of the act. She's what people come out to see."

"Next," Ronnie grumbled, "it'll be Carol Lee and the Whatevers."

"Not such a bad idea," said Bob.

"Ronnie and I write most of our songs," said Matthew.

"Songs are a dime a dozen," Bob told him. "Elvis hasn't written a song in his life. It's what he does with them that makes them hits. Speaking of which, if you guys had taken up my offer to be your agent, I'd already have inked a record deal for you."

They hadn't thought about that in a while. For six months, Matthew and Ronnie had been sending their tape to record companies. The latest one had kept it for over two months now, with no reply.

"Just to show you I've got your best interests at heart," said Bob, "I've invited a record talent scout to come out here tonight. But if you don't have an agent, he won't talk to you."

"Why not?" asked Matthew.

"He can't for legal reasons," was the reply. "So whaddaya say? I'll be your agent, just for the recording contract, for only 25 percent. Hey, I'm doing the work, right? And if you get nothin', then I get nothin'. Can't be any fairer than that."

The band members looked at each other. "I don't think it's a good idea," said Carol.

"I'd like to have a record," Matthew responded. "If we had a record, more people would hear us."

"Could get on the television too," said Ronnie.

"Look," said Bob. "I trust you kids. Let's just shake hands on it."

"We should call Aunt Lorraine," said Michelle.

"Listen, lawyers just slow things down," Bob explained. "We've already signed the contract she wrote for you. This is a different deal, and the talent scout will be here in an hour or two."

"Just for this one record, you'd be our agent, right?" Matthew asked Bob.

Bob shrugged. "If it's just for one, it's hardly worth my while. Maybe this guy would want you to sign up for a six-record deal. Maybe an album or two. It's only fair that I get paid for whatever I get for you."

Matthew looked at the others. "It's just for the records," he said. He held out his hand and Bob shook it enthusiastically. Then Bob stuck his hand toward Ronnie. "You and Matthew are the ones who write the songs, isn't that right? So I need the both of you."

"We *all* play on any record, though," Ronnie said.

"Sure, sure, I'll be happy to arrange anything you want."

Ronnie shook his hand.

"Now *that's* settled," said Bob. "You won't regret it. I got some phone calls to make." He went off toward his office.

"I don't think that was a good idea," said Carol. "And *we* should have had a say in it."

"Yeah, well, *we* didn't get any say when it became The Whatevers with Carol Lee," said Ronnie.

"It doesn't matter," said Matthew. "We're going to split the money five ways. It's just that we can't miss out on this chance."

"Carol's right," said Michelle.

"Nobody ever asked *me*," said Billy.

"Don't worry," Matthew said. He could feel the pressure building up within the band, and he didn't like it. "Everything will be OK."

That night, however, they were all feeling more nervous than they had in a long time.

They had gotten used to playing before the audience at Bob's. The leather jackets and tough looks didn't frighten them anymore. People came there now just to hear the Whatevers play, and the Whatevers knew it.

But tonight the band members were thinking about the talent scout. Would he be impressed enough? Carol and Michelle were still upset at the way their brothers took over the decision to let Bob be their agent. Billy DuPree was sulking because nobody had asked him, and he was thinking maybe he would just go off and start his own band.

Actually, Ronnie had started to regret shaking Bob's hand. Aunt Lorraine was probably right. Matthew was the problem, Ronnie thought. He wanted to have a record so bad that he was willing to do anything for it, even if it was stupid.

And Matthew—he had started to worry whether the band was good enough. Sure, it was good enough to play in this scuzzy little beer joint in Wisconsin. But so what? And Nell had liked them, but maybe that was a bad sign. Maybe they should have listened to Bernie, added some more instruments, smoothed out their sound.

He was still worrying about all that when Bob came on stage to introduce them. Bob was more enthusiastic than ever, building up the band: ". . . the sensation of the Chicagoland area, the biggest single rock-and-roll band in the Midwest and soon to start on a national tour . . . Bob's Dew Drop Inn presents The Whatevers!"

Bob turned, gave Matthew a wink, and pointed in the direction of the audience. Pretty clearly, the talent scout was out there someplace.

Bob had made up the "national tour" just to impress him.

As Matthew played, he stared past the footlights, trying to find the scout. But the room was so crowded and smoky it was impossible.

All at once, he noticed that the band wasn't playing the way it usually did. Nobody sounded right. Carol wasn't putting her heart into it. Billy sounded like his head was somewhere else. Michelle's saxophone playing wasn't lively any more. Even Ronnie seemed to just be going through the motions.

Chuck Berry

He turned to face them, and put some extra effort into his own playing. He jumped up and down the way he'd seen Chuck Berry do. That got their attention. They looked at him like he was going nutsy. "Let's go!" he yelled. Carol stumbled over a phrase in the song and nearly laughed.

It continued that way. For the rest of the set, Matthew played louder than the others—faster too, so that sometimes they didn't keep up with him. He knew it sounded awful, but all he could do was hiss at them between songs: "Follow me! Follow me!"

By the time the first break came, Matthew was sweating. Playing music had never been so hard for him before. He was ready to start yelling at the others when Bob came up the stairs to the stage, followed by another man.

Matthew froze. This must be the talent scout. And he had heard them on the worst night the band ever had.

Bob waved the others over. "This is Chuck Burnett," he said, "the guy I told you about."

Chuck had steely eyes. He looked like he didn't waste time. "You kids aren't too bad," he said, "except for the guitar player. You might think about replacing him."

Matthew felt like sinking into the floor. "Me? What was wrong with me?"

"You oughta listen to the rest of the group, kid. Sounds like you're playing at one speed and they're at another."

Carol spoke up. "We're not getting rid of Matthew."

"Uh, Chuck," Bob said, "the guitar player is Carol Lee's brother."

Chuck shrugged. "Oh, a family thing. But maybe get a second guitar player for the recording studio."

"We've already got a tape," said Ronnie. "We like what we did on there."

"Yeah? Where is it?"

Ronnie and Matthew looked at each other.

Both were thinking the same thing. Maybe it wasn't a good idea to let Chuck know they'd already sent the tape to a record company. "We don't have it with us," explained Ronnie. "But we can get it."

"Anyway," Chuck said, "we'll have to redo it with another guitar playing the lead."

Matthew bit his lip. Here was somebody else, like Bernie, who wanted to change the band. If people didn't like the music just the way it *was* . . .

"The guitar player is usually much better," said Carol.

That only stung Matthew even more.

"Now," Chuck went on, "we'll get you some songs to sing—"

"We have our own songs," said Carol. "Matthew and Ronnie wrote them." Actually Carol had helped too, but she said they could get the credit.

"Which ones?"

They told him.

"Yeah, well, 'It Doesn't Matter' could be your B side," said Chuck. "I know a couple of disk jockeys—important ones—who could give it some air play. But you understand the deal?"

"I'll explain it to them later," Bob interrupted.

"No," said Carol, "explain it now."

Chuck turned his steely eyes toward her. "I get songwriting credit and 50 percent of what the record makes."

All the band members were stunned. 'You mean . . . you'd get credit for writing *our song?*" said Matthew.

"That's the standard deal, kid," said Chuck.

"Yeah, it is," Bob added. "Everybody knows that."

"We don't know it," said Matthew.

"That's because you're *kids,*" said Bob. "That's exactly why you need an agent. And as your agent, I'm telling you to take the offer."

"Aunt Lorraine would never let us do that," said Ronnie.

"Yeah, well she can't get you a record deal either, can she?" said Bob. "This is between you and us. You can leave your Aunt Lorraine out of this."

"If you want to get to the big time," Chuck told them, "this is the only way to do it. Look, you'll make a lot of money just playing gigs as a band. If the record gets big, you'll be in demand. You could even get on television."

"I'm already on television," said Carol, "and it's not that big a deal."

Chuck looked at her again. He squinted. "I never saw you on television."

"You probably don't watch my program," she said.

Matthew motioned to Ronnie and they stepped off to one side.

"What do you think?" asked Matthew.

"I can't see it," said Ronnie. "We should check it with Lorraine."

"She'd say no," Matthew said.

"So why are you even considering it?"

"I don't know—Chuck's right in a way. If we had a hot record, we'd be somebody."

Ronnie smiled. "You'd still like to walk into school and hear kids singing your song, wouldn't you?"

Matthew nodded. That was it. It was just a dumb dream, but it was his. He took a deep breath. Oh well.

"Sorry," he said, when they rejoined the others. "We're not going to give away any part of our songs."

Chuck just turned away. "See you around," he said.

But Bob got a little bit angry. "Listen," he said, "part of this deal is mine, you know. You're turning down the chance of a lifetime, and 25 percent of it is mine. We had a handshake."

"It's like you said," Ronnie told him. "If we get nothin', so do you."

"After all I've done for you guys," Bob said bitterly.

On the way home, Matthew sat in the back seat wondering if it had been the right thing to do. It was true . . . Chuck wanted to cheat them. But maybe it was worth it to get cheated if it helped you move ahead. It wasn't just that he wanted to hear other kids sing his songs. He wanted them to listen to him play, listen to the music he had inside him.

Carol sensed what he was thinking. She put her hand on his knee. "Don't worry," she said, "we'll make it anyway."

Easy for her to say. She was already a television star. If Dad was right, she would have a singing career no matter how the band turned out.

When they got home, Matthew went to his room to get ready for bed. He was tired. He even wished they didn't have to go back and play at Bob's tomorrow night. It would just remind him of the chance he'd missed.

It was only after he turned on the light that he saw an envelope on his bureau. That was where Mom put any mail that came for him.

When he saw the return address, he forgot everything that had happened that night. The letter was from the last record company that they'd sent the tape to.

His hands tingling, Matthew ripped open the envelope. Just the first few sentences of the letter inside told him what he wanted to know. "We find your tape has commercial possibilities. We would be interested in releasing a recording with the two songs. If you would like to discuss contract terms . . ."

He ran down the hall to show the letter to Carol. "Do you think it's too late to call Ronnie?" he asked.

"Probably," she said. "But if I were him I'd probably kill you if you waited till tomorrow to call."

Our Kind of Music

OCTOBER 1957

ON THE DAY OF THE RECORD'S RELEASE, MATTHEW was up at 6:00 A.M. He couldn't sleep anyway, even though it was way too early for what he wanted to do. He planned to take the El down to Baker's music store, just to see if they had any copies.

The week before, he and Ronnie had gone to the store to ask them to order some. Old Mr. Baker had chuckled and said, "I got a couple dozen people a week come in and ask that. Some of the record companies even pay me to stock their records. What are you boys offering?"

They were taken aback. "Well, we think our songs are pretty good," said Ronnie.

"You know anybody who ever recorded a song they thought was *bad*?" asked Mr. Baker. But in the end he said if there was any interest in the record, he'd stock it.

Secretly, Matthew was hoping to hear the record on the radio. The promotion manager for the record company, a man named Leo, had told Matthew that was their best chance for getting a hit. Leo was a nice guy. "I hate rock and roll," he admitted with a smile. "But I know that kids will buy it. So what I've got to do is make sure as many kids as possible hear your record. But it's a chicken-and-egg thing."

"What's that?" asked Matthew.

"The radio stations play the Top 40 songs. Those are supposed to be the 40 songs that are selling the best in record stores. But the reason most kids buy a record is because they hear it on the radio. So which comes first? Was there an egg before there could be a chicken? Or did you need a chicken to lay an egg?"

Leo also told them that if you paid disk jockeys, they'd play your record on the air. "That's the best way to get started," he said.

But the band didn't have enough money to do that. Matthew asked his dad to lend them some, but he said, "This band nonsense isn't going to come to anything. People will have forgotten about rock and roll in a couple years. The only reason your Mom and I tolerate this band at all is because Carol talked Nell into that bargain."

"Carol's going to be too old for Nell's show in a year," said Matthew.

"Then, she can go into real music," Dad said. "Not this junk."

No matter what Dad said, rock and roll was catching on. There were now five stations in Chicago that played nothing but rock music. Leo said the record company had sent a promo record to each of them. As soon as Matthew got up, he was twirling the dial on the new transistor radio he'd bought. It ran on batteries and you didn't have to plug it in. He wished he had five of them so he could listen to all the rock stations at once.

By the time he left the house, though, nobody had played the record. Maybe later, he thought. Or tomorrow. Still, he would feel a lot better if he could hear it just once.

He and Ronnie had agreed to meet at the music store. Matthew held the transistor radio up to his ear on the El train. Still no luck.

The record store wasn't open when he got there. Sometimes Mr. Baker didn't arrive till 10:00. That was the way he was. Ronnie wasn't there either.

Matthew walked around the block to a Woolworth store. He sat down at the lunch counter and looked at the dried-up pies they kept in a glass case. Nothing looked good, so he ordered a cherry phosphate, his favorite drink. You couldn't get it in bottles. It had to be made at a soda fountain in a drugstore or five-and-ten. As Matthew watched, the soda jerk put some thick cherry syrup into the glass, then added a dash of phosphate and filled it with soda water. After stirring it, he passed the glass to Matthew.

Woolworth's lunch counter

A radio was playing on the shelf behind the counter. Matthew had just taken a sip of cherry phosphate when he heard Carol's voice:

It doesn't matter
What you do . . .

It took him a second to realize where it was coming from. He thought he was just hearing it in his head. Then, when he figured it out, he told the soda jerk: "Turn it up! Turn it up!" A couple of people sitting farther down the counter stared at him. The soda jerk didn't move. He was reading a magazine.

So Matthew took the transistor radio out of his jacket. Frantically, he spun the dial, trying to find the station playing the song. "What station is that?" he kept asking the soda jerk.

Finally he found it. He turned the sound up as loud as it would go. The speaker was so small that the music was distorted, but Matthew didn't care. He could hear the guitar playing—*his* guitar! On the radio!

He started to beat time on the counter with the hand that wasn't holding the radio. He looked around. Pretty clearly, everybody in the store thought he was crazy. The

A transistor radio

soda jerk had called the old uniformed guard who roamed the store trying to catch kids shoplifting.

"You'll have to turn that down, sonny," the guard said.

Matthew just smiled, stood up, and headed for the door, waving the transistor radio around so everybody could hear. He never finished the cherry phosphate, but he never forgot it.

That was the way it began. When he met Ronnie, the two of them went to Grant Park and spent the rest of the day listening for their song on the radio. In all, they heard it seven times. Each time, they jumped up and down and yelled like idiots.

At the end of the day they went back and told Mr. Baker that the song had been on the radio, and he said he'd already ordered three copies. "You'll need a lot more than three," they told him. They hoped they were right.

By the end of that week, they were sure of it. Every one of the five rock stations in Chicago was playing the song. One of the disk jockeys played it three times in an hour.

"They're getting requests from listeners," Leo told Matthew. "We're already getting re-orders from some record stores. And the song is on the radio in Cleveland, Philadelphia, and St. Louis too. How'd you like to bring the group into our studios to cut a follow-up record?"

This time, they brought Lorraine along. "Are you Ronnie and Michelle's mother?" Leo asked when he met her.

"No, I'm their aunt," she said. "I'm also the band's lawyer."

He did a double take. "Their lawyer? Are you . . ." He didn't finish the question.

"Sure am," she said. "U of Chicago Law School, class of '38."

"I just never met . . ."

"A Negro woman who was a lawyer?"

He smiled weakly. "But if you're their lawyer, hey, it's OK by me. We were thinking of giving the group, say $500 for their next record."

"Fifty thousand," Lorraine said.

Even the band members nearly fell out of their chairs when they heard that. As for Leo, he jumped up as if his pants were on fire.

But in the end, he agreed.

"How'd you know he'd pay us that much money?" Ronnie asked when they left the office.

"I called a few radio stations and found out how big your first record is," she said.

"Yeah, but . . . fifty thousand smackers! How'd you come up with that?"

"Somebody told me to start with a figure so crazy nobody would pay it."

"But he did."

Lorraine nodded. "I guess I'm not crazy enough."

She wasn't. As the first record spread across the country, other offers started to come in. Lorraine had called everybody down to her office for a meeting. Matthew's dad was there, along with Ronnie and Michelle's father, and Billy's mother. Even Nell showed up. "I feel responsible for them in a way," she said.

"Somebody wants the band to play at a concert in Cleveland," Lorraine said. She showed them a stack of telegrams. "And St. Louis, Pittsburgh, Indianapolis, and on and on."

"They can't go on that kind of tour," said Dad. "They're still in school."

"Freddy," Nell said to Dad, "they have a chance for a big career."

Before he could reply, Lorraine added, "We can arrange concert dates on weekends or in the summer. They wouldn't be working any harder than they are at Bob's. And they'll be earning a lot more money."

"They shouldn't be playing at that kind of disreputable place at *all*," said Dad. He had gone to see them at Bob's for the first time just two weeks ago.

"A tour would be good for the band," said Ronnie's father. "I'll cut my schedule short so I can travel with them."

Dad threw up his hands. Matthew knew that meant he would give in.

But Carol asked, "Why can't we just go on television?"

Lorraine frowned, and Nell spoke up. "I know that was mentioned earlier," she said. "And I spoke to some of the people I know in the business. After all, when Ed Sullivan invited Elvis Presley on his show, I thought all the doors must be open. But they're not."

"Why not?" asked Carol.

Dad burst in with the answer. "You have an integrated act."

"What does that mean?" asked Matthew.

The adults all seemed embarrassed.

"It means," said Lorraine gently, "that your skin colors are different."

"Don't you read the newspapers?" growled his dad. "Kids are so ignorant today."

Matthew did read the newspapers, a little. He watched the television news more. There had been a lot of stories about integration lately. Matthew understood what the word meant. "But," he said, "I thought that only had to do with schools."

"The schools are just part of it," said Ronnie's father. "There are people who don't want to see Negroes and whites together in any situation. So the national television networks won't show integrated acts."

"Haven't you noticed," Ronnie said, "that there aren't any Negro kids on *Howdy Doody*? Or *The Aunt Nell and Huckleberry Show*?"

Matthew turned red. He had never thought about it. It had just seemed . . . OK that all the kids on those shows were white.

"The network won't let us put any colored boys or girls on the show, dear," Nell told Ronnie.

Matthew looked at his dad, who worked for the network.

"Don't look at me like it's my fault," said Dad. "The sponsors have to sell their products in the South. Any sponsor of an integrated television show would lose sales." He spread his arms. "No sales, no sponsor, no show. That's just the way it is."

A bad feeling settled over the room. Matthew thought about the pictures he'd seen on the TV news. When a few Negro kids tried to go to an all-white high school in Little Rock, Arkansas, it had caused riots. A mob of people tried to attack them. The people in the mob were adults. After a few days, President Eisenhower sent in troops to keep the Negro kids from getting killed. Only after that did they get to go to school.

Matthew looked around the room. "I guess we've had just about everybody try to break up our band. Bernie said Carol couldn't sing. Chuck said I couldn't play the guitar—"

Little Rock High School

"We all knew that," interrupted Ronnie, "but we were too polite to say so."

Matthew laughed. "OK, see, they're saying now we can't play because we're the wrong colors. Are we going to let that stop us?"

Ronnie shrugged. "Never bothered *me* that you were the wrong color."

His sister Michelle looked across at him. She wasn't sure he was telling the truth.

Ronnie saw it. "OK, so it bothered me a little," he said. "At first. But I got over it." He shot Matthew a look, as if daring him to say something.

"I guess I got over it too," Matthew said. He turned to Lorraine. "We want to go to some of those places you mentioned. Ronnie and I will write some new songs. Can you arrange it so we don't get cheated?"

"I think so," she said. "But there are some places you can't go."

"No trips to Little Rock, huh?"

"Not *this* year."

Their first concert was in Indianapolis. They drove down in the red-and-white 1957 Chevrolet that Ronnie had bought with part of the money from their first record. Ronnie's father drove behind them in another car with the equipment, so they couldn't speed. "Nobody trusts us, do they?" said Ronnie.

"We're pretty dangerous, all right," Matthew replied. Ronnie put the top down, though, and

they liked the feeling of driving along with the wind blowing in their faces. They waved to kids on bicycles along the road.

A radio station in Indianapolis had arranged the show. It was going to be held in a band shell in a park. The disk jockey showed his surprise when he met them.

"You guys are the . . . ah, Whatevers?"

"All five of us," said Carol firmly.

"You couldn't tell on the record," said the disk jockey.

"What couldn't you tell?"

"Uh . . . that there are five of you."

"Anything wrong with that?"

"Hey, I don't care. It's just that nobody told me."

They all knew he really meant that they weren't all the same color.

Ronnie and Matthew got to work setting up. "If we ever make an album," said Ronnie, "are we gonna put our pictures on it?"

"Good idea," said Matthew. "Then people who see us won't be so surprised. How surprised do you think that guy will be when he hears our new song?"

"*Very.* Maybe we better get paid in advance."

It was a warm evening, even though it was October. The space in front of the bandshell began to fill up fast. Matthew was glad to see that the crowd was nearly all young people. Some of them sat on the concrete benches around the open-air theater. Others had brought blankets and spread them on the grass in front of the stage. He knew they'd like the music.

Back in Chicago, a newspaper reporter had interviewed Matthew after the band's first record became a hit. Matthew could tell that the man didn't like rock and roll, because his questions were kind of nasty. "How long do you think people will want to listen to this music? Why does rock and roll cause young people to become violent? Do you think that listening to it causes brain damage?"

But one of the questions Matthew answered pretty well. He'd been thinking about it himself, maybe ever since he first heard somebody call the music rock and roll.

The newspaper reporter asked, "What *is* rock and roll, anyway?"

Matthew took a breath. "Rock and roll is the kind of music people my age like. That's all it is." He crossed his fingers, thinking of Nell. "We don't know why old people don't like it, but they have their own music. Now we have ours."

As Matthew looked out over the crowd in front of the band shell, Matthew thought of that answer. The newspaper reporter, in his article, had called Matthew "an arrogant young man who seems determined to play this kind of so-called music until no one wants to listen any more. Which may be sooner than he thinks."

Well, that time hadn't come yet, Matthew thought. This was going to be the biggest crowd the Whatevers had played for.

It looked like a good time to try out their new song, the one he and Ronnie had just written.

Matthew didn't know that the song would make the band famous. He didn't realize that the record they made of it would be banned in towns across the country. Or that it would be held up as an example of the evil music that was corrupting American youth.

Nor did he know that all these things would make the song more popular. He couldn't have guessed that forty years later, radio stations would still be playing it and that people who were young in 1957 would still remember it. Because to them it stood for something new that their generation brought to the world.

The song would change his life, and the lives of everybody in the band. But none of them knew that as they prepared to play it for the first time. Ronnie's drums tapped out the beat, Matthew picked out the opening chord, and Carol stepped to the microphone to sing:

My parents don't understand.
My teachers aren't with it, no.
But you know what I know
Just what makes the world go.

It's love, L U V
It's love, L U V
That's what matters
Between you and me.

Don't care if you're white
Yellow or brown.
Even if you're red

You can be a friend of mine.
'Cause it's love, L U V
It's love, L U V
That's what matters
Between you and me.

A Few Historical Notes

During World War II, the United States and the Soviet Union had been allies in the effort to defeat Nazi Germany. After the war, the Soviets occupied much of eastern Europe and used their military position to establish communist governments there. The United States and the Soviet Union soon found themselves on opposite sides in a new war—the "Cold War."

Many Americans feared that Communists planned to overthrow the United States government as well. Congressional committees, in particular the House Un-American Activities Committee, began a search for American Communists. Congress was particularly interested in finding Communists in the entertainment industry.

It had never been illegal to belong to the Communist Party. Most who joined it in the 1920s and 1930s had done so out of idealism. Now they were asked by Congress to confess not only their past membership, but name others who had been Communists as well.

Some Americans protested that this Communist witch-hunt was a violation of rights guaranteed in the Constitution. However, those who refused to answer the committee's questions often lost their jobs, as described in our story.

In the 1950s, about the only thing feared and despised as much as communism was rock-and-roll music. From its roots in blues, soul, and country music, rock spread swiftly, having great appeal for young people. However, their elders condemned it. *Time* magazine wrote that the music was banned in many cities because "its primitive beat attracted 'undesirable elements.'"

The business dealings of the band called the Whatevers are not exaggerated. Many songwriters of the 1950s had to share the credit and profits from their songs in order to get them produced and played on the radio. Unscrupulous agents took large percentages of the money their young clients earned. Record companies often paid disk jockeys to get records played on the radio, which was a key to success.

Millions of Americans bought their first television sets in the 1950s. In the early days, local stations broadcast almost anything that they thought viewers might watch. In Cincinnati, Ohio, where one of the authors of this book grew up, one program showed only a hand drawing pictures on an easel while music played in the background. Journalists predicted that television was only a fad that would never replace movies. However, shows like Milton Berle's *Texaco Star Theater* (starting in 1948, renamed *The Milton Berle Show* in 1954), *I Love Lucy* (1951), and *The Honeymooners* (1955) attracted audiences of millions and made television the most popular entertainment medium of all time.

The Dixon Family

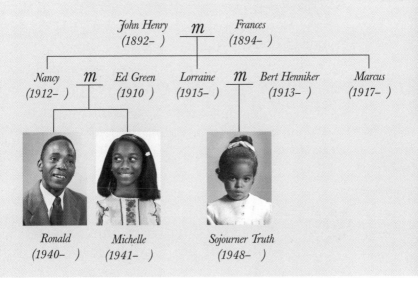

John Henry (1892–) **m** Frances (1894–)

Nancy (1912–) **m** Ed Green (1910) Lorraine (1915–) **m** Bert Henniker (1913–) Marcus (1917–)

Ronald (1940–) Michelle (1941–) Sojourner Truth (1948–)

The Vivanti Family

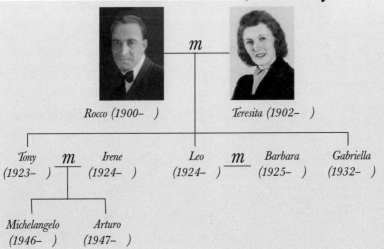

Rocco (1900–) **m** Teresita (1902–)

Tony (1923–) **m** Irene (1924–) Leo (1924–) **m** Barbara (1925–) Gabriella (1932–)

Michelangelo (1946–) Arturo (1947–)

The Aldric

Lionel
(1833–1902) m

Richard m Laura
(1866–1912) (1867–1912)

William m Anna
(1867–) (1868–)

Harry m Valerie
(1887–) (1919–)

Jack m Sara
(1888–) (1891–)

Peggy
(1889–) m Charles
Norman Sr.
(1888–1918)

Ne.
(1900

David Esther
(1924–1945) (1932–)

Dick
(1946–)

Charley
(1917–) m Jeanne
(1920–)

Charles III
(1947–)

Family

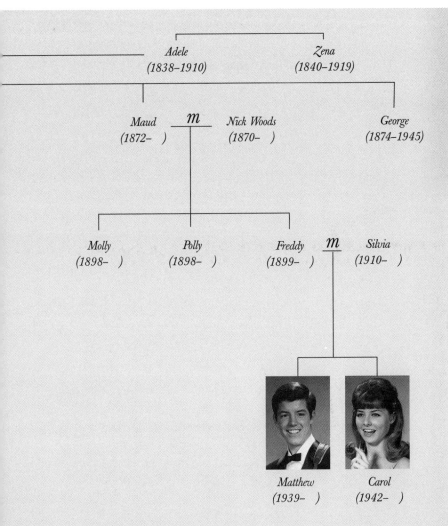

Adele
(1838–1910)

Zena
(1840–1919)

Maud
(1872–)

m

Nick Woods
(1870–)

George
(1874–1945)

Molly
(1898–)

Polly
(1898–)

Freddy
(1899–)

m

Silvia
(1910–)

Matthew
(1939–)

Carol
(1942–)

Things That Really Happened

1950

Senator Joseph R. McCarthy of Wisconsin claims that he has a list of 205 Communists working in the State Department. McCarthy does not reveal the names. This is the beginning of a series of similar accusations. His tactics become known as McCarthyism.

President Harry Truman orders U.S. air and naval forces to aid South Korea in defending itself against an attack by North Korea. He appoints General Douglas MacArthur to lead the defense forces.

Puerto Rican Nationalists attempt to assassinate President Truman.

The first Xerox copy machine is produced.

1951

Chinese Communist troops enter the Korean War in support of North Korea.

General MacArthur advises President Truman to attack China, and the president dismisses MacArthur as head of the U.S. forces. By the end of the year, the two sides in the Korean War have fought to a stalemate, and a truce is negotiated.

The first color television show is broadcast.

1952

General Dwight D. Eisenhower, running on the Republican ticket, defeats Illinois governor Adlai E. Stevenson in the presidential elections.

During the Years 1950–1959

During the campaign, Eisenhower's running mate, Richard M. Nixon, defends himself against charges that he has profited from a political expense fund. In a nationally televised speech, Nixon claims that the only gift he kept is a cocker spaniel named Checkers that was given to his daughters. The "Checkers speech" saves Nixon's political career.

The first three-dimensional movie, *Bwana Devil*, is shown in theaters.

Mad comic books go on sale for the first time. Later the format is changed to a magazine.

1953

Bermuda shorts for men become popular.

For the first time, more than half of all American families own a television.

1954

The U.S. Supreme Court rules that segregation is illegal in public schools.

After Senator McCarthy accuses the U.S. Army of harboring Communists, the Senate opens hearings into McCarthy's charges. Millions of Americans watch the nationally televised hearings. Later in the year, the Senate votes to condemn McCarthy for conduct "contrary to Senate traditions."

The silicon transistor is developed.

Swanson markets the first frozen-food "TV dinners."

Twenty-six comic book publishers adopt a code that restricts violent or vulgar content.

1955

Rosa Parks, a black woman, refuses to give up her seat to a white passenger on a Montgomery, Alabama, bus. The bus driver calls the police, who arrest her. Black citizens of Montgomery start a boycott of the bus line.

Disneyland opens for business.

The Wiffle Ball is developed.

1956

In Hungary, a rebellion breaks out against the Communist-dominated government. The Soviet Union sends military forces and tanks to crush the rebels.

President Eisenhower is reelected in a landslide victory.

The first enclosed shopping mall opens in Minneapolis, Minnesota.

Dick Clark becomes host of the Philadelphia television show American Bandstand, which features teenagers dancing to rock-and-roll songs. The following year, the show is picked up by the ABC network.

1957

Mobs of whites prevent the entry of black students at Central High School in Little Rock, Arkansas. President Eisenhower sends troops to enforce the Supreme Court's integration order.

October 5, the Soviet Union launches *Sputnik*, the first satellite to orbit the earth. The Soviet scientific achievement causes many Americans to question whether the American school system is adequate.

1958

The United States launches its *Explorer* satellite in a bid to catch the Soviets in "the space race."

Alaska becomes the forty-ninth state.

The hula hoop becomes popular.

A grand jury in New York investigates television quiz shows that have provided questions or answers in advance to favored contestants. Later, all the networks drop prime-time quiz shows such as *The $64,000 Question* and *21*.

1959

Hawaii becomes the fiftieth state.

The first Barbie dolls are sold.

Rock-and-roll stars Buddy Holly, Richie Valens, and J.P. Richardson ("The Big Bopper") die in a plane crash near Clear Lake, Iowa, on February 3.